"Wha[...] ass I'm about to stomp."

"My name's Runt Rawls," said the smaller of the two, "and you won't forget it after tonight."

"Mine's Toughnuts," said the other one, and he swung a big fist at Slocum's jaw. Slocum blocked the punch and drove a punch into the man's gut. Toughnuts whoofed out air, but he stood his ground. As soon as Toughnuts swung, so did Rawls, and Cash just as deftly blocked his first punch. Almost simultaneously, Cash and Slocum swung blows that caught the men on their jaws, and the two thugs staggered backward to lean against the bar. Toughnuts was the first to move away from the bar, and he came at Slocum with his head down and both fists ready for action.

DON'T MISS THESE
ALL-ACTION WESTERN SERIES
FROM THE BERKLEY PUBLISHING GROUP

THE GUNSMITH by J. R. Roberts

Clint Adams was a legend among lawmen, outlaws, and ladies. They called him . . . the Gunsmith.

LONGARM by Tabor Evans

The popular long-running series about Deputy U.S. Marshal Long—his life, his loves, his fight for justice.

SLOCUM by Jake Logan

Today's longest-running action Western. John Slocum rides a deadly trail of hot blood and cold steel.

BUSHWHACKERS by B. J. Lanagan

An action-packed series by the creators of Longarm! The rousing adventures of the most brutal gang of cutthroats ever assembled—Quantrill's Raiders.

DIAMONDBACK by Guy Brewer

Dex Yancey is Diamondback, a Southern gentleman turned con man when his brother cheats him out of the family fortune. Ladies love him. Gamblers hate him. But nobody pulls one over on Dex . . .

WILDGUN by Jack Hanson

The blazing adventures of mountain man Will Barlow—from the creators of Longarm!

TEXAS TRACKER by Tom Calhoun

Meet J.T. Law: the most relentless—and dangerous—manhunter in all Texas. Where sheriffs and posses fail, he's the best man to bring in the most vicious outlaws—for a price.

JAKE LOGAN

SLOCUM'S
REVENGE TRAIL

JOVE BOOKS, NEW YORK

THE BERKLEY PUBLISHING GROUP
Published by the Penguin Group
Penguin Group (USA) Inc.
375 Hudson Street, New York, New York 10014, USA
Penguin Group (Canada), 90 Eglinton Avenue East, Suite 700, Toronto, Ontario M4P 2Y3, Canada
(a division of Pearson Penguin Canada Inc.)
Penguin Books Ltd., 80 Strand, London WC2R 0RL, England
Penguin Group Ireland, 25 St. Stephen's Green, Dublin 2, Ireland (a division of Penguin Books Ltd.)
Penguin Group (Australia), 250 Camberwell Road, Camberwell, Victoria 3124, Australia
(a division of Pearson Australia Group Pty. Ltd.)
Penguin Books India Pvt. Ltd., 11 Community Centre, Panchsheel Park, New Delhi—110 017, India
Penguin Group (NZ), 67 Apollo Drive, Rosedale, North Shore 0632, New Zealand
(a division of Pearson New Zealand Ltd.)
Penguin Books (South Africa) (Pty.) Ltd., 24 Sturdee Avenue, Rosebank, Johannesburg 2196,
South Africa

Penguin Books Ltd., Registered Offices: 80 Strand, London WC2R 0RL, England

This is a work of fiction. Names, characters, places, and incidents either are the product of the author's imagination or are used fictitiously, and any resemblance to actual persons, living or dead, business establishments, events or locales is entirely coincidental.

SLOCUM'S REVENGE TRAIL

A Jove Book / published by arrangement with the author

PRINTING HISTORY
Jove edition / December 2007

Copyright © 2007 by The Berkley Publishing Group.
Cover illustration by Sergio Giovine.

All rights reserved.
No part of this book may be reproduced, scanned, or distributed in any printed or electronic form without permission. Please do not participate in or encourage piracy of copyrighted materials in violation of the author's rights. Purchase only authorized editions.
For information, address: The Berkley Publishing Group,
a division of Penguin Group (USA) Inc.,
375 Hudson Street, New York, New York 10014.

ISBN: 978-0-515-14385-0

JOVE®
Jove Books are published by The Berkley Publishing Group,
a division of Penguin Group (USA) Inc.,
375 Hudson Street, New York, New York 10014.
JOVE is a registered trademark of Penguin Group (USA) Inc.
The "J" design is a trademark belonging to Penguin Group (USA) Inc.

PRINTED IN THE UNITED STATES OF AMERICA

10 9 8 7 6 5 4 3 2 1

If you purchased this book without a cover, you should be aware that this book is stolen property. It was reported as "unsold and destroyed" to the publisher, and neither the author nor the publisher has received any payment for this "stripped book."

1

Slocum had been on a long, hard ride. He had been across the desert and over tall-grass prairie. He had been through more small, one-horse towns than he had ever believed existed. He was amazed at how people would find an out-of-the-way place and build a fucking town there, for no apparent reason. He had run across several of those places. He was hunting a man. When he came across the son of a bitch, he meant to kill him. Kill him dead. Kill him once and for all. The man needed killing. He had done Slocum dirty, and Slocum's only purpose in life for the time being was to get the son of a bitch. He had been after this bastard for a long stretch now. He was hot and dusty and hungry and thirsty. He was thirsty not just for water. He wanted a drink of good bourbon whiskey. It would be really nice to have a room with a soft bed, a bottle of good whiskey, a pocket full of cigars, a steak dinner, a warm bath, and a warmer woman. All of that would be good, but all of that would wait. It would wait until Slocum had finished this task, this self-appointed job for no pay, this mission, currently his primary mission in life.

He knew he was on the right trail, for the story was always the same. Such a man had been in town not long ago.

His description was easy enough. He was a man of average height and build, nothing particularly noticeable about him, except his clothes. He always wore black. Everything about his clothing was black. Tall, black shiny boots, black trousers, black belt, black shirt, black vest, black jacket, black hat. His gun belt was made of black leather. Even his two guns were black. All black. Slocum figured that his long underwear must be black as well. His horse and saddle were black. His hair was dark brown. Slocum thought that must have been a source of major frustration to the man. He wore it long, down on his shoulders, and he wore a handlebar mustache. It was as if he were trying to look like Wild Bill Hickok. He was easy to describe and easy to spot. And Slocum was not far behind him.

The country was rough, Texas's hill country, and it was sparsely settled. The day was getting short with the sun low in the western sky. Slocum topped a rise and looked ahead. There was no sign of human life in front of him. He did spot a grove of trees down below and to his right. It looked to be a likely spot to spend the night, so he urged the tired Appaloosa onward. It was a bit cooler in the grove. The grass was green, and water trickled out of the hillside to form a clear pool. Slocum dismounted and unsaddled the big stallion, allowing him to drink and graze freely. Then he rolled out his blankets on the ground.

He pulled off his shirt and his boots and went to the stream to wash his face and to drink. Then he went back to his blanket and lay down for a much-needed rest and hopefully a good night's sleep. His Colt and his Winchester were close by his side. He was about to doze off when he heard the sound of approaching hoofbeats. He eased the Colt out of the holster and cocked it. In another moment, a rider came into the grove.

"That's close enough, mister," Slocum said.

"Whoa! You damn near scared the shit out of me, pard. I didn't know no one was in here. Didn't see no fire."

"I never built one," said Slocum. "It ain't cold, and I ain't cooking."

"Say," said the stranger, "I need me a place to camp for the night. There ain't a better site anywheres around here. What say you let me climb down and we build us a fire. I got some fresh venison here. Got some coffee too. Be glad to share it with you."

Slocum thought for a moment. He did not like the idea of sharing his campsite with a stranger, but the thought of fresh-killed deer meat and coffee appealed to him in a real compelling way. "Come on in," he said, but he kept his Colt in his hand. The stranger moved in a little closer and dismounted. In a few minutes, they had a fire going and meat cooking. The coffee was boiling in a pan. Slocum sat on one side of the fire with his Colt still in his hand.

"You're a mighty cautious one," the stranger said.

"It pays," said Slocum. "I'm alive."

"Yeah, well, this coffee's about ready, I'd say. Have a cup?"

"Thanks."

The stranger poured a tin cup full and reached across the fire toward Slocum with it. "Just put it down there," Slocum told him, and the man did. Slocum picked it up with his left hand and took a tentative sip. It was hot, but it was damn good. The stranger poured a second cup for himself. In a few more minutes, the meat was cooked, and the stranger parceled it out. Slocum ate heartily. By this time, he had laid his Colt on the ground beside him, but he kept an eye on the stranger as he ate. He was beginning to think that the stranger might be all right.

When they were done with the meal and had drunk all the coffee they wanted, they let the fire burn itself down. The night was warm, and they had no more need of it. Slocum told the stranger where to throw out his blanket, and watched carefully as the man prepared his bed. Then both men stretched out for the night.

It was late, and Slocum was asleep, but he was a light sleeper. He heard the sounds of the stranger saddling his horse. He opened one eye to watch. The stranger packed up all his belongings and seemed ready to hit the trail. Well, that would be all right with Slocum. But then, as Slocum watched him, the stranger took up Slocum's saddle and moved to the big Appaloosa. The spotted stallion snorted and backed away. The stranger hesitated, looked back at Slocum, then turned to the horse again.

"Hold on there," he said in a low and soothing voice. "I ain't going to hurt you, big fella. Come on now. Ease up."

As the stranger moved toward him again, the Appaloosa again backed away, and again he snorted, this time louder than before. There was no doubt now regarding the intentions of the stranger. Slocum picked up his Colt and thumbed back the hammer. The stranger stopped still at the ominous sound.

"Now, hold on there," he said. "This ain't at all like what you think it is."

"You tell me then," said Slocum.

"Well, I was just—"

"On second thought," Slocum interrupted, "just climb on your horse and ride away from here."

"Yeah. Sure. I'll do that."

The stranger dropped Slocum's saddle to the ground, but as he turned toward his own saddled horse, he went for his gun. Slocum pulled the trigger. The roar of the Colt in the grove of trees filled the still night, and the stranger jerked. His eyes opened wide as his fingers relaxed, and the gun dropped from his hand. Then his knees buckled, and he fell forward on his face.

Slocum stood up and walked over to check the body, but he knew that the man was dead before he touched him. He tucked the Colt into his britches and walked over to the stranger's horse to begin unsaddling the animal. "It ain't your fault," he told it as he dropped the saddle to the ground. Then he took off the bridle and tossed it aside. "Maybe you can find some strays or wild horses around these parts to play with." He took the stranger's blanket and threw it over the body, and then he went back to bed.

In the morning, Slocum rebuilt the fire. He boiled some more of the man's coffee and heated up what was left of the venison. When he was all done, he scraped out a shallow grave and buried the stranger. Then he saddled the Appaloosa, mounted up, and headed on toward the next town. This part of the country was full of hard cases. He knew it—he had just met one—and he knew that he had to stay ready for them.

He rode away most of the rest of that day, and when it was getting toward evening again, he saw the town ahead. Maybe, he thought, this will be the one. He figured that he had about enough cash for one good night in town, so when he rode in, the first thing he did was find the stable. He paid in advance and told the man to take particularly good care of the Appaloosa. Then he walked out and down the street to the first hotel he found. He got himself a room for the night, pocketed the key, and went out again. It was a small town, so it did not take long to find the saloon. He went in and ordered a shot of whiskey. The bartender was not too busy, so Slocum delivered the lines that had become standard with him, giving the bartender the description of the man he was hunting.

"There was a feller here," the barkeep said, "couple of days ago, I think. He fit that description pretty good."

"Two days ago?" Slocum asked.

"I believe so."

"He head on south, did he?"

"Can't say," the barkeep answered. "I seen him when he come in here. I never watched him leave."

Slocum finished his drink, went back to the hotel, and had a good night's sleep. He woke up the next morning and checked what was left of his cash. Just enough for a breakfast. He decided to use it that way. A full belly would make it a lot easier to hit the trail again. He got dressed and went out to find a diner, and he had a good breakfast of steak and eggs. After he had paid for it, he had one dime left. He slapped it on the counter for a tip, then walked out of the place.

He stood on the board sidewalk for a moment thinking. He wanted to be back on the trail. The man he was hunting was still two days ahead of him. But he knew that he wouldn't get too far without any cash in his jeans. For one thing, he was low on bullets, and that was the one thing he could not afford to do without. He pondered his situation. Then he walked back to the stable.

He got his Appaloosa saddled and ready to go, but before mounting up, he turned to the grizzled stable hand. "You know of anyone around here that could use a good hand? Just temporary."

"For what?"

"Most anything. I'm traveling, and I'm broke. I'd like to stop for a short spell and get some more money in my jeans before I head on."

"Orvel Patterson out at the Switchback just got hisself a string of new horses," the man said. "I don't know, but maybe he could use someone to gentle them up some."

Slocum got directions from the man, then rode out toward the Switchback. It was a short ride from town, and Slocum noticed upon reaching it that it was a neat and clean spread. He rode straight up to the main house, and as he drew close, a man about fifty stepped out the front door. Slocum touched the brim of his hat.

"Howdy, stranger," said the man. "What can I do for you?"

"I'm looking for Orvel Patterson," Slocum said.

"Well, you found him."

"Man in town told me that you got some new horses you

might need some help with. I just need some temporary work is all."

"What's your name?"

"John Slocum."

"You a bronc buster, Slocum?"

"I have been. Could be again."

"You feel up to showing me?"

"Now?"

"You know a better time?"

"Right now is just fine," said Slocum.

"Follow me."

Patterson led the way around the house to a corral filled with horses. "See that roan over there by the fence?" he asked.

"Yeah."

"You get that son of a bitch ready for me to ride into town this afternoon, and you got the job."

"I'll take him on," Slocum said. He took the rope off his saddle and paid out a loop. Then he climbed over the fence and began easing his way toward the roan. The horse saw him coming and kept moving away, but Slocum kept after him. He had to move in between the other horses, all nervous by this time. At last he saw his chance, and he tossed his loop. As it snugged around the neck of the roan, the horse began to rear and whinny and stomp. Slocum quickly lashed the other end of his rope around one of the fence posts. He let the roan carry on for a while.

There was an adjacent corral, separated from the first by a gate, and Slocum moved to open the gate. He began waving his hat and yelling, and in a few moments, he had all the other horses driven into the adjacent corral. He shut the gate, and then he turned back to the roan. It was still jerking its head and pulling at the rope. Slocum moved to the rope and caught hold of it, pulling it toward himself. When he got a little slack, he lapped it around the post.

In a short while, he had the roan snubbed up tight against the fence post. He found a saddle and blanket and bridle and soon had the creature ready to ride. Well, he at least had it ready to try to ride. He moved in close to its head as he took up the reins. "Now, listen here, ole pardner," he said. "You and me are fixing to have us a ride." He mounted up quickly, and then he loosed the rope from around its neck and tossed it aside. Immediately, the roan leaped forward. Slocum hung on.

The animal kicked up its heels in an attempt to throw Slocum over its head, but Slocum stuck. It fishtailed. It reared. It jumped high in the air and came down hard on all fours, jarring everything in Slocum's body. But Slocum stayed in the saddle. When it had done all the bucking and jumping it could take, the horse started running in fast circles around the corral, and it tried to rake Slocum off its back by scraping the fence. Even then, Slocum stayed stuck. At long last, the roan was worn out.

Slocum rode it around and around the corral at a walk. He turned it this way and that. He stopped it, and then he made it go again. He talked to it as he did these things. Finally, he rode to the fence where Patterson stood waiting and watching. He patted the horse on the neck and looked down at Patterson.

"You did say you just wanted temporary work, didn't you?" Patterson asked him.

"That's right."

"You'll do," said Patterson.

Slocum unsaddled the roan and turned it loose. Then he followed Patterson to the bunkhouse. Patterson showed him where to stow his gear and where he would sleep.

"Work at your own pace," he said. "I'll pay you for each horse you break, not by your time."

"All right," Slocum said, "but I won't be lazy."

He was thinking about the trail he was following, and he knew that the more time he took with the horses, the farther ahead his prey would get. He couldn't allow the man to get too far away from him. He stashed his gear and walked back to the corral. Now and then, cowhands stopped by the corral to watch him and cheer him on. Occasionally, he caught a glimpse of Patterson watching, but mostly the old man was off doing something else. No one cowhand stood around for too long at a time. It seemed to be a pretty smooth-running outfit. Everyone knew his job and stayed busy with it.

Slocum rode down three more horses before he was called to lunch. The cook was good too, and Slocum really enjoyed his meal. He ate all he could hold, recalling all those long and hungry days on the trail. In a way, he was glad to have that other thing nagging at him, for if he had nothing else to do, he might hate to think of having to give up this job. Actually, he wouldn't have wanted to keep this job for long. He was really thinking of an ordinary cowhand's job. Busting broncs was rough work. He was already feeling sore. Well, he would just have to live with it for a while, till he could line his pockets some.

When lunch was over, he was back at the corral again. He tackled four more of the brutes that afternoon, and again, he only quit when he was called to dinner. He thought the lunch had been good, but the dinner was even better, and he was beginning to get acquainted with some of the hands. They seemed like a pretty nice bunch of boys, and Slocum had noticed that old Patterson ate in the cookhouse with the crew. He wondered if the old man was a bachelor or just a hell of a democrat.

When dinner was over, Slocum headed for the bunkhouse. A young cowboy called Saddler stepped alongside him. "You're doing a heck of a job out there, Mr. Slocum," he said.

"You can drop the mister," Slocum said, "and thanks."

"I never seen anyone ride like that."

"It comes with practice," Slocum said. "You worked here long?"

"A few months."

"I guess old Patterson is a bachelor, huh?"

"Well, he's a widower, I guess you call it," Saddler said.

"He live alone in that big ranch house?"

"He's got a niece living there with him. His sister's daughter, I think."

"How come he eats with the crew? Or how come she don't?"

"Oh? I get it. He don't usually eat with us like that. Beverly, that's his niece, she's off visiting somewhere just now. Ordinarily, they eat together in the big house."

"I see," Slocum said.

"What you planning on doing for the rest of the evening, Mr.—uh, Slocum?"

"I'm hitting the hay early," Slocum said. "Those damn broncs have got me plumb sore all over."

2

It had all started some time earlier when Slocum had been riding a trail in northern Colorado. He had just come from a job with some small ranchers who were bucking the system of the big ranchers and their political cronies, and he was not feeling real great. While he couldn't say that he had been on the winning side, neither could he say that they had won. Somehow, after some people had been killed on both sides, the small ranchers managed to keep their spreads, but none of the big boys ever got prosecuted. It stunk as far as Slocum was concerned.

He was riding the trail south, and he came across a scene that churned his guts. A small gang of cowhands had a man on horseback, hands tied behind his back, sitting under a big oak tree with a noose around his neck. It sure as hell looked like Judge Lynch was at work, and coming from the kind of scene he had just been through, Slocum did not like it a bit. It made him think of the big ranchers he had been working against. His first impulse was to ride down among the cowhands and challenge them, but he decided that would be foolish. They outnumbered him. Likely, he'd get himself shot dead or maybe even beaten senseless, only to share the same fate as their intended victim.

11

The trail Slocum was riding was up on a high hill, and it was cluttered with boulders on either side. The hanging was taking place down below in a valley. Slocum had a sudden thought. He dismounted and, taking his Winchester, moved behind one of the big boulders. He cranked a shell into the chamber and took aim across the top of the boulder. It would not be an impossible shot. Carefully, he sighted in on the rope just where it lay over the branch of the tree. He had made more difficult shots. One of the men in the gang below raised a quirt, and Slocum squeezed the trigger.

The horse neighed and jumped forward. The man in the saddle leaned back, and the rope snapped. Horse and rider ran ahead at full speed. The gang of would-be hangmen looked around in panic. Each of them pulled a gun. Slocum fired a second shot into their midst, and they scattered. He watched and waited till he was sure that they had all gone in another direction; then he mounted up and rode after the man with the noose around his neck.

It took some hard riding, but Slocum managed to catch up with and stop the runaway horse. Amazingly, the man was still in the saddle, his hands still tied behind his back and the noose still around his neck. Slocum reached over to untie the man's hands. His hands free, the man pulled the noose from around his neck and tossed it aside. "You came along just in time, friend," he said. "Was it you that cut that rope?"

"It was my shot," Slocum said.

The man stuck out his right hand, and for the first time, Slocum took note of the man's appearance, all black clothes and shoulder-length hair. A handlebar mustache under his nose. Slocum took the hand and squeezed it.

"I'm Joe Cash," the man said. "You've just made a friend."

"John Slocum."

"Say, Slocum, how come you did that anyway? We don't know each other, do we?"

"Far as I know," Slocum said, "I've never seen you before today. I just didn't like what I saw back there. That bunch looked like a lynch mob to me."

"That's just what the bastards were," Cash said. "They accused me of rustling. They never caught me with their cows and never tried to take me to the sheriff. Just decided to hang me."

"I know their kind," Slocum said. "Where you headed, Cash?"

"I wasn't headed anywhere till those bastards decided to hang me. Now I guess I better move along."

"I'm riding south," Slocum said.

"South sounds good to me."

They rode together after that. The trail led to one small town after another, and they stopped at each one to spend a night or two, get some good meals and maybe a whore each for a night. Then they rode on. They had no destination in mind other than the general direction "south." Then they stopped at a place called Hell Town. It didn't look like much, but it did have a saloon. They tied their horses just outside its front door and went inside. At the bar, they ordered themselves drinks. While the barkeep was setting up the drinks, Cash said to Slocum, "I don't know about you, ole pard, but I'm getting tired of dusting my britches on that trail. I think we ought to look for a place to set a spell."

"Find a job?" Slocum said.

"That sounds reasonable. Don't you think?"

"Well, if we don't do something like that," Slocum said, "I'm going to be plumb broke real soon."

Cash put some coins on the counter to pay for the drinks. Over at a nearby table, a man stood up. He looked to be in his forties, maybe older. He wore a suit and a mustache. He walked over to the bar to stand beside Cash.

"Pardon me, boys," he said.

Slocum and Cash looked at the man.

"My name's Townsend. I own a spread outside of town.

I didn't mean to be eavesdropping, but I heard what you just said about looking for work. Were you serious?"

"Yeah," Slocum said.

"It depends on the work," said Cash.

"I'm just looking for good hands," Townsend said. "A hard day's work for a fair day's pay. I have a good cook and a clean bunkhouse. A pretty good bunch of boys. What do you say?"

"You'd take a chance on a couple of strangers?" Slocum said.

"You look like good, seasoned hands to me," Townsend said. "Tell me your names, and we won't be strangers."

"I'm John Slocum."

"Joe Cash."

"Well, boys, come on over and sit at the table with me. I'll buy you another drink."

Slocum and Cash took their glasses with them and moved to the table with Townsend, who poured their glasses full from a bottle he already had sitting on the table. It was better whiskey than what they had been served at the bar. While Slocum and Cash sipped at the good whiskey, Townsend told them a bit more about the jobs: what the hours were like, how much he paid and when. Then: "Well, will you take the jobs?" he asked.

"I've been on ranches where the boss said if a man works for him, so does his horse. No one but me rides my horse," Slocum said.

"That's all right with me," Townsend said.

Cash looked at Slocum. Then he looked back at Townsend and stuck out his hand. "Sounds good to me, Mr. Townsend," he said. "We'll take them."

Townsend shook Cash's hand and said, "Hell, just plain ole Townsend will do fine. Glad to have you."

Then he shook Slocum's hand. "Now, boys," he said, "the first thing I'm going to ask you to do is just sit here and drink with me tonight on account of that's what I come into town to do. When we get sloppy drunk, I'll pay for you to have a room tonight. In the morning, we'll head on out to the ranch. How's that suit you?"

"That suits us just fine," said Cash.

Townsend was no cheapskate. He bought good whiskey, and he bought plenty. In a while, a saloon girl came to their table. Townsend told her, "Hell, honey, I'm too old for that, but maybe one of these boys might be interested." Cash smiled real big, reached up, and took hold of the gal's arm. She smiled back and sat on his lap.

"What's your name, honeypot?" Cash asked.

"You just said it, cowboy."

"What? Honey Pot?"

"That's it. What do I call you?"

"Cash will do just fine."

"Well, Cash, do you want to go upstairs with me?"

"And get some Honey from out of your Pot?"

"I think you got the right idea."

Cash picked up his drink and drained the glass. Then he put the empty glass on the table. "Well, Honey Pot, let's go," he said. They got up and headed for the stairway, and Townsend poured his own and Slocum's glasses full again. "I hope he ain't had too much whiskey to have a good time up there," he said.

"He'll likely have himself a good time," said Slocum. "Honey Pot might not, though."

Townsend laughed and took a good sip of whiskey.

Honey Pot and Cash were at the top of the stairs. She was holding tight onto Cash's arm, and she led him down the hall to a room with an open door and then on into the room. She turned loose of his arm long enough to shut the door, and then she took him on over to the bed. Cash reached his arms around her, pulled her in close to him, and kissed her on the lips. Breaking loose at last, Honey Pot began to undo her clothing. Cash took off his gun belt, refastened the buckle, and hung it up on the head of the bed. Then he started pulling off items of clothing as fast as he could and tossing them aside.

He was naked before Honey Pot, and he started helping her to get undressed. At last, she moved onto the bed, spread her legs apart, and reached her arms toward Cash. For a moment, he stood looking at the glistening, slightly damp, blond hairs that grew over her snatch. Then he moved on top of her, and she circled his body with her arms. They kissed again. Honey Pot reached with both hands underneath Cash's body to find his rod stiff and ready for action. "Ooohh," she moaned as she guided it into her already wet hole and then thrust upward with her pelvis. Cash responded with a downward thrust. His entire length was inside her channel.

"Ah," he said, pulling back slowly until only the head of his swollen cock was still buried in her pussy. Then he thrust it back inside her as she shoved upward. Their movements were slow for a few more thrusts, but Cash got anxious. He began pumping furiously, and Honey Pot responded in kind. The mattress creaked, and the headboard banged against the wall rhythmically.

"Ah, ah, ah," Honey Pot moaned.

"I'm going to come," said Cash.

"Let me have it," said Honey Pot.

A sudden surge of hot juice spurted from Cash's cock into the depths of Honey Pot's lovely love tunnel. Cash continued thrusting a few more times. At last he relaxed, still lying on top of her, his cock slowly growing softer inside her. Then it slipped out by itself, and slowly he rolled over to lie beside her on the bed.

"God damn," he said.

"You like that?"

"Oh, Honey Pot, you were just fine."

They stayed like that in silence, except for heavy breathing, for another couple of minutes, and at last Honey Pot asked him, "Do you think you can go again?"

"I don't know, Honey Pot," he said. "You might have taken all I had."

She rolled over and kissed him on the lips, a long and lingering wet kiss. Then, she slid down a bit to kiss and lick his chest and his nipples. He moaned with pleasure and anticipation. Her hands sought his still-wet and sticky cock and fondled it, one moving down to cup his balls. He groaned again. "You're damn sure welcome to find out for yourself," he said. She moved down lower and, gripping his limp cock in one fist, kissed it on the head. Cash flinched. "Oh," he moaned. Honey Pot licked it. "God damn," said Cash. Honey Pot then started licking it all over. She licked until she cleaned the cock off.

Then suddenly, she opened her mouth wide and sucked the head in. Cash's cock grew hard again, and he thrust it upward. Honey Pot took it all in. She bounced her head up and down, slurping along the length of his hard tool. Cash began breathing hard again, and every now and then, he moaned. All the while, Honey Pot's hands stroked his thighs and played with his balls. Finally, she pulled off long enough to ask him, "Do you want me to finish you off like this?"

"Oh, no, Honey Pot," he said. "It's good, but why don't you move over on your hands and knees?"

"Ooh," she said. "I like that."

She was positioned in a quick moment, and Cash was up on his knees behind her. As he moved his engorged rod into position, Honey Pot reached back with one hand between her own legs, found it, and maneuvered it into her slimy slit. "Oh, yes," she said. "Give it to me, baby. Ram it in."

Cash did not need to be told twice. He pounded himself over and over into her round, white ass. He could see her titties shake and bounce with each thrust. Honey Pot lowered her head and shoulders to the mattress, leaving her smooth ass poking upward, and Cash pounded harder and faster.

"Fuck me, Cash," she cried out. "Fuck me hard."

"Yeah," he said. "Yeah. Take that. Take that."

Cash finally slowed down. He was panting for breath. This second go-round, he was lasting much longer than the first. He made a few slow thrusts, then a few faster ones. "You want to lay down and let me get on top?" Honey Pot asked. Cash pulled out and flopped over onto his back. Honey Pot quickly straddled him, took hold of his throbbing cock, and once again guided it into what was by now her sloppy wet hole. Then she sat down on it, taking the entire length up inside her. She rocked forward on her ass and moaned with pleasure.

"Oh, cowboy," she said, "I could ride you like this all night."

She rocked faster and faster, until she cried out with pleasure and delight and fell forward to lie against Cash's chest. She kissed him on the mouth with her lips parted wide, and her tongue shot into his mouth and licked around. Then she straightened up and began rocking again. She came at least a dozen more times until at long last, Cash's tool had done all the work it could. He felt the pressure building up in his heavy balls. He was thrusting upward with each of her forward motions. He thrust faster and faster, and she did too. Then suddenly, he gushed forth.

"Oh," she said. "My God. You're filling me up."

But then she could feel much of it running back out and down onto his belly and legs. He felt it too. They were both perspiring heavily too after all that action. Honey Pot lay down on him again, wrapped her arms around him, and rolled them over so that he was on top. Cash made a few more feeble thrusts, and she responded, but then he went limp again. His cock slipped free. He started to move off her, but she held him tight.

"Stay there for a while," she said. "Just relax. I like to feel your weight press down on me."

"You're quite a woman, Honey Pot," Cash said.

"You ain't so bad yourself, cowboy," she said. "You feel like you got your money's worth?"

"And then some."

"Cash," she said, "you was so damn good, I almost feel guilty taking your money."

"I ain't paid you yet."

"Well, notice that I said 'almost.'"

"I did catch that, Honey Pot," he said.

Downstairs, Slocum and Townsend sat in the same chairs they had occupied since Cash and Honey Pot had gone upstairs. The bottle was getting low. Townsend picked it up and refilled both glasses. That was it. He waved an arm at the bartender. "I think we better have another one," he said. Just then, Honey Pot and Cash appeared at the top of the stairs arm in arm. As they started down, Townsend said, "Yeah. Just in time too."

3

All three men were slow getting around the next morning. They spoke little, moaned a lot, and dressed slowly. At last, in a little eating joint, they ordered up huge breakfasts and lots of coffee and ate voraciously. Finally done with their meals, they sat over a last cup of coffee. Townsend, all of a sudden, was a new man. He put down his cup with a loud sigh.

"God damn it, that's better," he said. "How are you boys?"

"Like you said, Townsend, better for the breakfast," Cash replied.

"Just fine, Townsend, just fine," said Slocum. "Are we headed for the ranch this morning?"

"Right now," said Townsend. "If you're done with your coffee."

"Raring to go," said Cash.

In a few minutes, they were mounted up and riding the trail. Cash said to Slocum, "You missed out on a real hot one last night, ole buddy. You just didn't speak up fast enough."

Slocum was thinking that he did not care to sleep with whores. He preferred not to pay for it, and he had seldom

21

found that necessary. Oh, he had done it a few times, but for the most part, when he had a woman, she wanted him as much as he wanted her. He had always found it better that way. He kept those thoughts to himself, though, and said, "Well, maybe I'll learn if I keep watching you."

Cash laughed out loud. "You do that, ole pard. You just keep your eyes on ole Cash. You'll learn a lot."

"That's a damn fine-looking Appaloosa you're riding, Slocum," Townsend said, changing the subject. "I can see why you said what you did about no one else riding him."

"It ain't just that," said Slocum. "He won't let anyone else sit on his back."

"How long have you boys been riding together?" Townsend asked.

"Not long," Slocum said.

"We, uh, just kind of happened across each other's trail a few days ago," Cash added, and he gave Slocum a sly look.

"You seem to have hit it off pretty well," said Townsend. "That's good. Men who get along with each other work better together. You'll find that I've got a good bunch of boys out at my place. You'll like them all right."

It was another two hours before they reached the ranch. They saw to their horses, and then Townsend took them to the bunkhouse and introduced them around. He showed them where to stow their gear and where they would sleep. Then he walked with them back over to the big house. As they were approaching it, the front door opened and a young woman stepped out. She stood watching them with her head cocked to one side.

"Julie," said Townsend, "I just hired these two men. This here is John Slocum."

Slocum touched the brim of his hat.

"And his pard here is Joe Cash. Boys, this is my niece, Julie Townsend."

"Hello, boys," Julie said with a half smile on her lips.

She was young and pretty, with auburn hair hanging over her shoulders.

"Well, how do you do, ma'am," said Cash, taking off his hat and giving a slight bow. "May I say that you're a real sight for sore eyes?"

"Thank you," she said, and she turned and walked back into the house.

Slocum noticed Townsend shoot a hard look at Cash. "What do you want us to do, Townsend?" Slocum asked.

"The barn needs cleaning out," said Townsend. "Think you can handle it?"

Cash started to protest, but Slocum jabbed him in the ribs. "We'll get on it right away," he said. He took Cash by the arm and turned him, and together they walked toward the barn. After a few steps away from the boss, Cash said, "Cleaning out a barn ain't proper work for cowhands."

"When a man pays you for a day's work," said Slocum, "you do what he wants done. And you watch yourself around that gal."

"Did you take me on to raise, Slocum?"

"It damn sure seems like it just now."

Cash laughed. The two men spent the rest of that day cleaning the barn. At noon and later at supper, they met the rest of the ranch hands, and that night, they hit the hay in their new bunks. They were up early, feeling a bit stiff from the work of the day before. They were seated at the long breakfast table with the rest of the crew when Townsend came up. He issued a few orders to the foreman, Shotgun Stone, and then he turned to Cash and Slocum.

"There's a stretch of fence over on the east side of the ranch that needs fixing," he said. "Can you handle it?"

Slocum gave Cash a kick under the table. "We'll take care of it," he said.

The fence turned into a two-day job. There was some post-hole digging and a lot of wire stretching. Cash grumbled and cursed most of the time. Once, Slocum said, "What's your problem, Cash? You said yesterday that cleaning out a barn ain't no work for a cowhand. You ain't thinking the same thing about mending fence, are you?"

"Ah, hell," Cash said, "I figured we'd be out in the saddle riding herd, rounding up strays. When Townsend offered us this job, he didn't say nothing about needing a couple of damn laborers. He said cowhands, didn't he?"

"I believe the man's exact words were, 'I'm looking for a couple of hands. A hard day's work for a fair day's pay.' That's the way I recall it."

"Ah, shit. You know as well as I do that what he meant to say, and he implied it pretty clear, was that he needed cowhands. Now, damn it, Slocum—"

Just then, the wire he was stretching snapped, and the barbed end took out a piece of Cash's left ear. He yowled and slapped at the side of his head.

"Damn it," he said. "Damn it. Now that's the last straw. That's the last fucking straw. I'm riding out of here right now."

"It's been good knowing you, Cash," said Slocum. "Don't pick up any stray cattle on the trail. I won't likely come riding up at just the right time again."

"You ain't coming with me?"

"I like the job just fine," Slocum said.

"Well, shit," said Cash, turning up the palm of his gloved hand to look at the blood in it. "How much of my damn ear's missing?"

Slocum grinned. "It appears to be all there," he said. "That wire just nicked it a bit is all. Ears bleed real easy."

"Hell, maybe I'll stick another day."

At the end of their third day of work, the barn was clean and the fence was mended. "I wonder what dirty job ole Townsend's got for us tomorrow," Cash said. "Maybe he needs a new shit hole dug."

But in the morning at breakfast, after Townsend had given his orders to Shotgun Stone, he added, "Have Slim and Hoss take Slocum and Cash along with them over to the west pasture."

"Sure thing, boss," Stone said.

Cash looked at Slocum and grinned. "Well," he said, "it's about damn time."

For the next several days, they rode the west pasture. It was rough country, marked by gulleys and washes, with scattered patches of brush all around. A low and slow-moving creek ran through the middle, and it was lined with more brush and occasional cottonwood trees. The very far western edge was rugged and rocky hills. The four cowboys combed this tough country gathering strays to bring back to the main herd. It was hot and dusty work, but Cash did not complain. It was real cowhand work, and he liked it. Slocum took note that Cash rode well, and he could handle a rope.

At the end of a long day, they were riding back toward the bunkhouse, eager for the meal that would be awaiting them. "This suit you better than mending fence, does it?" Slocum asked.

"Hell, yes," said Cash.

"You've done a share of this kind of work," said Slocum. "It shows."

Cash grinned and wiped sweat from his forehead with his bandanna. "Hell," he said, "I started it when I was fourteen. I had to. My old man, he was drunk all the time. He hadn't always been like that. I can recall when he was a hardworking son of a bitch. I don't know what happened, but he got to drinking—too much. He lost his job, but he found money somewhere to buy his damn booze. I went to work to pay the rent and buy the groceries. That worthless bastard would've just let Mama and me starve to death and never even noticed. I worked for an outfit called the Double R Bar over in the Panhandle."

"I've heard of it," said Slocum.

"It was a good place to work. Close to home. Mr. Reynolds that run the place was a good man to work for too. 'Course, he's gone now. I don't know who's got the place anymore. My old man got killed in a saloon. I worked on for Mr. Reynolds for another couple of years after that."

"What happened?"

"Mama died."

Slocum figured that was a good place to stop asking questions. He figured that maybe the young kid had decided that it was time to drift. He'd heard the story before: a youngster drifting from one ranch to another. Cash certainly was not alone in that. They didn't talk much for the rest of the ride back to the bunkhouse. But when they had cleaned up and sat down for their evening meal, they ate hearty, just like the rest of the crew. As they headed for the bunkhouse, a young cowhand called Monkey walked up beside Cash.

"I sure do admire the way you ride and rope, Cash," he said.

"Yeah?"

"I ain't seen many like you. Did it take you a long time to learn?"

"I don't hardly recollect, kid," said Cash. "I guess it did take a while, though. Say, but you're doing all right. You'll get there."

"I don't know. I try real hard, but I just can't seem to get the hang of it like you got it."

"Just be patient, kid."

"I can sit my horse all right," Monkey said. "But the way you swing that rope—well, I just don't see how you do it."

"Ah, you—say, we still got a couple of hours before we need to turn in. Get your rope."

Monkey looked at Cash with wide eyes.

"Go on, kid," said Cash. The kid took off at a run. Slocum slapped Cash on the shoulder.

"You do have a soft spot, you ole son of a bitch," he said.

"Ah, go to hell, Slocum," Cash said.

Slocum watched for a spell while Cash showed Monkey some of the finer points of roping. He showed him how to pay out a loop, how much slack to keep in the rope, and where and how to swing his loop. That went on for the next few evenings, and the kid was getting better. Cash was a good teacher. One evening, as Cash came late into the bunkhouse, Slocum said, "You're doing a good job with that kid, Cash. His roping has improved considerable."

"Ah, hell, Slocum, he's a natural."

"I'll admit to being a bit surprised you taking up with him the way you did."

Sitting on the edge of his bunk, Cash pulled off a boot and dropped it to the floor. "He reminds me of myself," he said. "At one time."

In a couple of days after that, they had a night off, and most of the hands rode into Hell Town for a night of drinking and whoring at the saloon. Monkey rode in with Slocum and Cash. Inside the saloon, the three cowboys bellied up to the bar, and Cash called for a bottle and three glasses. The barkeep brought them, but he looked at Monkey and said, "You sure this one's old enough?"

"How old he is ain't none of your business," Cash said. "He's with us."

He paid the man and poured three drinks. Monkey picked his up and looked at it. "Cash," he said, "I never drunk whiskey before. Truth is, I ain't old enough."

"Sure you are, kid. Drink up."

Monkey tossed down the whiskey all at once and immediately began to choke. The other men at the bar all started to laugh. Cash pounded Monkey on the back. Finally, Monkey quit hacking. He straightened up and took a deep breath. "Oh," he said. "That was good."

The laughter was even louder then. Cash grinned and poured Monkey's glass full.

"Have another," he said.

"But this time," said Slocum, "sip it."

Just then, Honey Pot stepped up to Cash's side and put a hand on his shoulder.

"I was wondering if I'd ever see you again," she said.

Cash swept her into his arms and gave her a big kiss.

"I'm back, Honey Pot."

"Wow," she said. "I can see that."

"Barkeep," Cash called out. "Another glass."

The bartender brought the glass, and Cash suggested that they all find themselves a table. There was an empty one near the foot of the stairs, and so they all moved to it and sat down. Cash poured all four glasses full.

"So how've you been, cowboy?" Honey Pot asked.

"Working like hell," Cash said. "Say, Honey Pot, I want you to meet my pardners here. You know Slocum?"

"I recall he was here with you the last time," she said. "Glad to meet you, Slocum."

Slocum tipped his hat.

"A pleasure, ma'am," he said.

"And this here is my newest pard, Monkey."

Monkey's face was burning red. He took off his hat and nodded his head. "Yes, ma'am," he said. "It's a real pleasure."

There were cowboys in the place from nearby ranches, and two of them at the bar got into a fight. They were soon put out into the street, and several others followed along to watch. Monkey was beginning to weave in his chair. He tried to remain calm and collected, but the booze was getting to him. He didn't think that anyone noticed, though. He picked up his glass and took another sip.

Honey Pot leaned in close to Cash's ears and whispered in it, "You want to go upstairs, cowboy?"

Cash started to get up. Then he settled back down. "That sounds like a damn good idea, Honey Pot," he said, "but I think maybe it'll wait for something important. I got me an idea."

"What is it?"

"I think that Monkey here needs to get his first taste of sweet honey. What do you think about that?"

"I'm just the girl who can take care of that little problem," Honey Pot said. "You want me to take him upstairs?"

"Right now," Cash said. "While he can still walk."

"You got it, sweetheart," she said, standing up. "Maybe you'll come along later?"

"Bet on it."

Honey Pot walked over to Monkey and took him by the arm. He looked up at her, almost startled.

"Come with me, cowboy," she said. "I'm going to take good care of you."

Monkey looked from Honey Pot to Slocum to Cash, and Cash said, "Go on, kid. It's all right. Hell, it's better than all right."

Slocum watched as Monkey and Honey Pot mounted the steps together. Then he looked at Cash. "Are you sure about this, Cash?" he asked.

"Never more sure about anything, Slocum. Hell, that boy will thank me for the rest of his life."

4

Honey Pot shut the door behind them as she and Monkey went into the room. Monkey stopped and stood still. He took the hat off his head and held it in both hands in front of himself. His face was red. Honey Pot had already started to unloose her bodice when she noticed. She stopped what she was doing and walked up to the young cowhand. His eyes were staring at the floor.

"Hey," she said. "It's all right." She took his hat from him and hung it on a hook on the wall. "Just relax. I ain't gonna hurt you."

"I'm—I'm sorry, ma'am," Monkey said. "It's just that I—"

"Hey, I know. You don't have to say nothing, and you don't have to do nothing you don't want to do. Come on over here and sit down with me. Okay?"

"Yeah. Okay."

Honey Pot took Monkey by the arm and led him to the bed. She sat on its edge and gently pulled him down beside her. "You okay?" she asked him.

"I'm okay."

"You ain't never been with a woman before, have you?"

31

Monkey's blush turned deep red. "No, ma'am," he said. "I ain't."

"Well, that's all right. There's a first time for ever'thing and for ever'one. Ain't nothing to be ashamed of."

She held his hand, and he felt a chill run over his entire body.

"You want to kiss me?" she asked.

"I'd like to."

Honey Pot put a hand on Monkey's cheek and turned his head toward her. Then she kissed him on the lips, gently and briefly. She backed away just a little. "That wasn't so bad now, was it?"

"No, ma'am. That was just fine."

She kissed him again, this time longer, and he responded passionately. This time when she broke away, she said, "You can stop that ma'am stuff, kid. I'm Honey Pot." She pressed her lips once more against his, and this time they parted. Her tongue snaked in between his lips, and he opened them to let it roam free.

Slocum and Cash had themselves another drink. Slocum glanced toward the landing at the top of the stairs, and Cash noticed. "Quit worrying about that kid, Slocum," he said. "What the hell's wrong with you anyhow? You forgot your first piece?"

"I ain't forgot. I just hope that kid's ready for everything you're introducing him to. That's all."

"There's only one way to get ready, and that's to jump right in. Hell, pard, he'll be all right. Quit worrying and have a good time. You ain't a good nursemaid nohow."

Slocum grinned and picked up his glass for a sip of whiskey. As he lowered the glass, he said, "I reckon you're right, Cash. I'm acting like an old woman."

Just then, two cowboys walked in through the front door. They swaggered as they stepped up to the bar and shouted for whiskey. They were types that Slocum had seen before, too many times. Braggarts and bullies, they were troublemakers. He could tell at a glance. Well, let them make their trouble. It was none of his business. He noticed that they wore their sidearms low. They obviously thought that they were gunslicks too. Someday, someone would show them different. He picked up his whiskey glass and drained it, then poured it full again.

In the next few minutes, the two bullies came close to starting two fights, but each time the person they picked on showed good sense and backed off. They continued to laugh and talk loud in general, challenging the whole world to a fight. Slocum suddenly wanted to get out, but he thought about the boy upstairs, and he could just see Cash getting himself into trouble with those two. Cash could handle himself. That wasn't a problem. But if the kid happened to come down and get into the middle of it, well, that would be a different story. He told himself that he had to hang around for a while longer.

Upstairs, Monkey was on top of Honey Pot and pumping away. He was panting with each thrust of his hard dick into the depths of her luscious cunt. "Oh, yes, baby," she said. "Oh, yes. You're doing great. You're wonderful. Keep it up, big boy."

Monkey shoved into her again, and then he felt it coming. "Oh," he shouted. "Oh, God."

He pumped his juices into her again and again, continuing his thrusts all the while. At last he was spent. He lay down hard and heavy on her and gasped for breath. Honey Pot stroked his back. "You done real good," she said.

"Was I all right?"

"Honey, you were more than all right. You're as good as any man I ever had, and believe me, I've had plenty."

"God, do you really mean it?"

"I mean it. I ain't gonna tell you that I never lie to a man, but I ain't lying to you. You done me real good."

"God, Honey Pot," Monkey said, "I'm glad."

"Do you think you could go again?"

Sometime later, Monkey and Honey Pot appeared on the landing. She was hanging on to his arm, and he was grinning like a possum. Honey Pot caught the look that Cash shot in her direction, and she smiled knowingly. When they reached the bottom of the stairs, they headed for the table where Cash and Slocum still sat drinking. As they sat down, Cash looked at Honey Pot and said, "Well?"

"Well what?"

"How'd the boy do?"

"He done just fine. Don't you worry your head none about this boy."

Cash laughed out loud and slapped Monkey on the back. "So how was it, kid?"

"Cash, I'm in your debt. It was—well, it was great."

Slocum drained his glass again and said, "I think it's time we headed back for the ranch."

"What's your hurry?" said Cash.

"Come on," Slocum said.

"Well, shit, you go on if you've a mind to, but me and the kid here is staying. The night's young, pard. There's whiskey to drink and women to lay. You getting old or what?"

That was a hell of a thing for Cash to say. All of a sudden, Slocum did feel very old. He wanted no part of this life, but at the same time, he did not want to leave the two cowboys, especially Monkey. Something told him that if he left them there, Cash would get Monkey in trouble. He'd never forgive himself if the kid got hurt. "Shit," he said, "drink up and let's get out of here."

"Hey," said one of the two braggarts at the bar. "You two fellers there got yourselves a genuine nursemaid, it sounds like. Better let him take you on home and tuck you in bed."

"He ain't my nursemaid," said Cash. "I'm staying here till the place closes down."

"Come on, Cash."

"I've had my say."

"Cash?" said the man at the bar. "Is that your name? Cash?"

Cash stood up and faced the man. "I'm Joe Cash," he said. "You got any problem with that?"

"No. Hell, no. It's just that, if you're Cash, you ought to have the moneybags and you ought to be telling the nursemaid what to do. You better just go on home with him. You and the kid."

"They've been trying to start a fight with someone ever since they came in," said Slocum. "Leave them alone. Let's just get out of here."

Slocum stood up, but the tough at the bar walked over to block his path. His buddy walked over to stand beside him. "Say, nursemaid," the loudmouth said, "your two pards don't want to go. You hard of hearing? Why don't you just go on out of here by yourself and leave them be?"

"Why don't you two go back to the bar and mind your own business?" Slocum said.

"I'm making it my business," said the man.

"Yeah. Me too," his companion said.

Slocum heaved a sigh. Joe Cash stood up. Monkey started to stand, but Cash said, "Sit still, kid. There's two of them and two of us." He walked a half circle around the table to stand beside Slocum.

"What's your names, boys?" he said. "I like to know whose ass I'm about to stomp."

"My name's Runt Rawls," said the smaller of the two, "and you won't forget it after tonight."

"Mine's Toughnuts," said the other one, and he swung a big fist at Slocum's jaw. Slocum blocked the punch and drove a fist into the man's gut. Toughnuts whoofed out air, but he stood his ground. As soon as Toughnuts swung, so did Rawls, and Cash just as deftly blocked his first punch. Almost simultaneously, Cash and Slocum swung blows that caught the men on their jaws, and the two thugs staggered backward to lean against the bar. Toughnuts was the first to move away from the bar, and he came at Slocum with his head down and both fists ready for action.

Rawls turned slightly, picked up a bottle from the bar, and smashed it, leaving the neck and jagged edges in his hand. He moved toward Cash with this new weapon at the ready. Toughnuts swung both fists hard and fast, most of his blows missing or landing on Slocum's shoulders. One lucky punch snapped Slocum's head back, but he quickly retaliated with a hard right to the side of the man's head, sending Toughnuts staggering back again.

Rawls lunged at Cash with the broken bottle, but Cash sidestepped just in time, and kicked Rawls in the ass as the man moved past him. The kick sent Rawls forward, where he ran into an empty table and sprawled over it. Cash ran after him and, before Rawls could get back to his feet, grabbed him by the belt and slung him the rest of the way over the table and down onto the floor.

Toughnuts rushed at Slocum, and Slocum stepped aside and hit him hard on the back just between the shoulders, knocking him to the floor. He reached down and pulled Toughnuts to his feet by the shirt collar, turned him around, and smashed a right into his jaw. Toughnuts staggered back again, but this time, Slocum kept moving. He moved in and struck twice more, and Toughnuts collapsed.

In the meantime, Cash waited for Rawls, who had lost his broken bottle, to get back to his feet. Rawls looked around. He saw that his partner was down and beaten. He looked at Cash and at Slocum, and he hesitated. Slocum sat down.

"Don't worry about me," he said. "I'm done."

Rawls put up his fists and moved hesitantly toward Cash. Cash waited, his fists poised too, but as Rawls came close, Cash delivered a swift kick to his balls. Rawls doubled over, his face turning green. He fell onto the floor, both hands gripping his groin, and rolled over and over moaning and groaning. Cash dusted off his hands and moved back to the table to sit down again.

"Damn, Cash," said Monkey, "that was a hell of fight. You too, Slocum. Both of you. You whipped them real good."

"You boys made some bad enemies," said Honey Pot.

"Those two?" Cash said. "Hell, we can handle them any day."

"Not just them," she said. "The whole White Hat outfit. They're a mean bunch, and they stick together. It won't be comfortable for you three in town after tonight."

"Why three?" Cash asked. "The kid didn't have anything to do with it."

"He's your pard."

"Well, anyone wants to make a fight of it, they're welcome," said Cash.

"That goes for me too," Monkey said. "I ain't a-skeered of them. Cash and Slocum made me stay out of this one. It woulda been three against two. Otherwise, I'd a been right in there with them."

Toughnuts struggled to his feet just then and staggered to the bar, still bent over. He leaned on the bar and hollered for whiskey. Rawls moaned another time or two. Then, seeing that his partner was up and drinking, he helped himself to his feet by hanging on to a chair. He did not straighten up, though. He stood doubled over, still holding his balls. His face was still a pale green. Slowly, he hobbled to the bar next to Toughnuts. Soon, both men had glasses of whiskey, and they drank them down fast.

"Are you two ready to go yet?" Slocum asked.

"Naw, hell, Slocum," said Cash, "the trouble's all over with. We might as well stick around now."

About that same time, Toughnuts whispered to Rawls, "You ain't hurt too bad, are you?"

"Son of a bitch like to of mashed both my balls," Rawls whined back.

"Didn't mash your gun hand, did he?"

Rawls turned his head to look Toughnuts in the face. "My gun hand ain't hurt," he said.

"Get ready then," said Toughnuts. "When I tell you, we'll turn on them. You take the one that kicked your balls, and I'll take the other one."

"What about the kid?"

"He won't be no problem once them other two is out of the way."

Slocum stood up just then. "Well, I've stayed around here too long already," he said. "If you two are damn fool enough to stay longer, it ain't my problem."

"Where you going, Slocum?" asked Monkey.

"I'm going back to the ranch. If you've got any sense, you'll come along with me."

Monkey gave Cash a look, and said, "What about it, Cash?"

"Hell, let him go, kid."

"We'll see you later, Slocum," said Monkey. "Don't worry. We'll be all right."

Slocum headed for the door, and Toughnuts said to Rawls, "Now." Both White Hat men went for their guns. Slocum heard the call, and he whirled. His Colt came out as he turned, and as it leveled on Toughnuts, it barked. Toughnuts's shot went into the floor. He stood still, looking down at the bloody hole in his chest. His mouth dropped open. His hand relaxed, and the gun slipped from his fingers. Then he fell forward on the floor and lay still—dead.

At almost the same moment, Cash, who was still seated, flung himself over backward. When he hit the floor, he rolled to his right, and he pulled out his six-gun. Rawls fired twice. His first shot went right where Cash had been sitting. His second dug into the floor just where Cash had rolled. He did not get a third shot. Cash pointed his gun and fired. The slug tore into Rawls's forehead, and the man's head bounced crazily on his shoulders as his body relaxed, then crumpled into a wad.

"Damn fools," said Slocum. He holstered his Colt, turned, and walked on out the door. Cash picked up his chair and sat down again. He and Monkey and Honey Pot sat for a moment in silence.

"Well," he said finally, "I reckon Slocum might be right, kid. It might be time for us to go on back."

Monkey was staring at the two bodies on the floor. "Yeah," he said.

"Just one thing, boys," said Honey Pot. "Ain't no question about it now. You're all in big trouble."

5

First thing the next morning, Slocum walked over to the big house. As he was climbing the steps to the front porch, the door opened and Julie Townsend stepped out. Slocum stopped, surprised, and took the hat off his head.

"Good morning, Mr. Slocum," Julie said.

"Morning, ma'am," said Slocum. He realized that he was staring at her, and he forced himself to look down at the steps. "I, uh, just came over to have a word with Mr. Townsend."

"He'll be out in a moment. Won't you sit down?" She indicated one of several chairs that were scattered around the porch. Slocum climbed the last two steps and went over to the chair to sit. He waited until Julie was seated.

"Thank you, ma'am," he said.

"How do you like your job here so far, Mr. Slocum?" Julie asked.

"The boys are all friendly enough," Slocum said, "and Mr. Townsend seems to be a fair man."

"You didn't really answer my question."

"A job's a job. If a man had enough money in his jeans, he wouldn't need one."

"So you don't have enough money?"

41

"I ain't never seen enough money, ma'am."

"Well, Mr. Slocum, you're certainly not going to get rich working here."

"No, ma'am."

The door opened again, and Old Man Townsend stepped out. When he saw Slocum sitting with Julie, he looked up a bit surprised. "Oh," he said. "Good morning, Slocum. Don't you have an assignment?"

"Yes, sir, I do," said Slocum, standing up. "But I wanted to have a word with you."

Julie stood up then and said, "I'll just be going back into the house. Excuse me, gentlemen."

Townsend shot her a glance, and Slocum said, "Morning, ma'am."

"Well," said Townsend after the door had shut behind his niece, "what is it?"

"Mr. Townsend, last night in town, me and ole Cash killed a couple of White Hat boys. Does it matter?"

"It might."

"Well, they picked a fight with us. We was minding our own business, sitting at a table with young Monkey and that gal Honey Pot. They was standing at the bar, and they come all the way over to us to pick a fight. We told Monkey to keep out of it, and he did. Well, we whipped them pretty good, but as I was leaving the place, they went for their guns. Both of them. Me and Cash was just faster than them is all."

"How come you're telling me this, Slocum?"

"I thought you might want to tell us to ride on." Slocum waited for a response from Townsend, but there was none. He continued. "Honey Pot said the White Hat is a pretty tight outfit. We might bring trouble on you."

"You thinking you ought to run for your life, are you?"

"It ain't that, Mr. Townsend. I don't want to bring my trouble on you is all."

"Slocum, go find your partner, and you might just as

well bring Monkey along. Get back over here with them right away. We'll have us a talk."

Slocum stared at Townsend for a moment, wondering what the old man was up to. Then he put his hat on. "All right," he said. "We'll be back in a hurry."

As Slocum went down the steps, Townsend stood watching him go. In another moment, Julie stepped back out on the porch and walked over to stand beside her uncle. She gave him a curious look.

"It's started, Julie," he said. "Do you want to catch the stage back East?"

"No, Uncle," she said. "I'll stick it out."

Slocum returned, followed by Cash and Monkey. He had told them of his conversation with the old man, and they were ready for anything. When they reached the house, they found Townsend sitting on the porch alone, waiting for them. "Come on up, boys," he said. "Have a chair and a cup of coffee." He gestured at a table with a tray of cups and a coffeepot on it.

"We'll hear what's on your mind first," said Cash.

"Well, sit down then."

They all sat. No one said anything more. They were waiting to see what Townsend had to say. He poured himself a cup of coffee and took a sip.

"Boys," he said, "I hired you—well, not you, Monkey. You were already here. I hired you two under false pretenses. I led you to believe that I was needing cowhands. Truth is, I thought you looked like gunslingers. That's how come I hired you."

"What?" said Cash, leaning forward in his chair.

"You heard me right. I've been expecting trouble with the White Hat outfit for some time. When I first saw you two, I was afraid that you might have come to town to work for them. When I heard you talking about looking for jobs, I made you an offer before you got a chance to go the other way."

"You're paying us cowhand wages," Cash said.

"If you'll stay on with me," said Townsend, "that'll change."

Cash leaned back and rubbed his chin. "Well, now," he said. "What about the kid?"

"He's a cowboy," said Townsend. "He's no gunfighter."

"He will be," Cash said. "I want him with us."

Townsend looked at Monkey. "What do you say, son?"

"I go with Cash, Mr. Townsend."

"All right. Slocum?"

"You say you been expecting trouble with that bunch?"

"For quite a spell. Aw, we've had a few fights in town, but they haven't amounted to much. Not till last night. Now, I'm afraid that it will all break loose. Well, what do you say?"

"I don't like being suckered into a situation," Slocum said.

"I been paying you to be a cowhand," Townsend said. "I didn't start that fight last night. You can ride out if you've a mind to."

"I'll stay on," said Slocum. "At cowhand's wages."

"You crazy?" said Cash.

"I hired on to be a cowhand," said Slocum. "If trouble comes, I'll fight."

Guy Hembree rode his horse hard, harder than he should. He whipped it up as he turned into the main gate of the White Hat Ranch, riding underneath the arched sign overhead that bore the emblem of a big Stetson, also the brand of the outfit. Guy rode hard till he arrived at the ranch house, a low, rambling building with an overhanging roof in front but with no porch underneath it. As he pounded up to the house, the door opened and three men stepped out, curious to see who was driving a horse so hard. One of the three men stepped out in front as Guy dismounted.

"What are you doing, Guy?" the man asked. "Trying to kill my horse?"

"No sir, Mr. Amos. I ain't. I just got urgent news from town is all."

"Well, what is it?"

"Rawls and Toughnuts're dead," Hembree said.

"What?"

"Killed. In the saloon."

"Who did it?"

"I don't know their names, but they work for Townsend. There was three of them in the saloon together. One of them just sat there while the other two done the job. To tell the truth, Toughnuts started the fight. Them two beat the shit out of them. Then one of them, he headed for the door. Rawls and Toughnuts went for their guns, but the other two was faster. Much faster. Jesus. I never seen anything so fast."

"So you're telling me that it was a clear case of self-defense. Is that right?" Amos asked.

"Yes, sir. I'm afraid so."

"They were that fast?"

"Yes, sir."

"So Townsend's got himself a couple of gunfighters, has he? Well, we'll see about that. Stackpole."

One of the two men with Amos stepped up to his side. "Yeah, boss?"

"I want you to go to town. Poke around. See if you can find out the names of those two."

"Yeah, boss." Stackpole headed for the corral to get a horse.

"In the meantime," said Amos, "we'll hit them where they ain't expecting it. Hank, you and Guy here, I want you to do a little job tonight."

"What is it, boss?" asked Hank.

"Take a couple more boys with you. Tonight, just after dark, ride onto old Townsend's north pasture. I know he's

got a small bunch of cows up there. There might be a cowhand or two over there watching them. Might not be. Kill
all the cows and all the men you see."

"Just like that?" asked Guy.

"Just like that," said Amos. "Townsend started it up.
Let's get it on."

Slim and Hoss were riding in the north pasture. They were
not riding together. Slim could see Hoss across the way until the sun dropped below the horizon. Then he lost sight of
him in the dark. He rode slowly around the small herd,
watching for any signs of trouble. Everything was quiet.
Besides that, he did not expect any trouble. There had been
no rustling in the area for several years, and the trouble
with the White Hat hands was all confined to fights in
town. He was alert, but he wasn't worried. He rode easy.

Hank and Guy, with four other hands from the White Hat,
topped the horizon, and from their vantage point, even in
the darkness, they could see both of Townsend's riders.
They stopped for a moment to survey the scene below them.
Then Hank said, "Guy, you take those two with you. Go
over to the left. Take out that cowhand there, and then start
shooting the herd. We'll go to the right and do the same."

"Got you," said Guy.

The group split up and rode off in opposite directions.
Soon, Guy's bunch was riding down hard on a surprised
Hoss. Too late, Hoss jerked the six-gun out of its holster.
Shots zipped past him on both sides. Three bullets hit him
almost at once in the chest and belly. Hoss fell from the
saddle dead. His horse fell an instant later. Then the raiders
started shooting cattle.

Across the way, Slim heard the commotion. He pulled out
his six-gun and yelled out, "Hoss!" He started to ride in
Hoss's direction, but then he saw the other group headed for

him. He snapped off a couple of wild shots, then turned to run. He could see he was outnumbered. He had no idea what had become of Hoss. He wanted to stay and fight, but he also wanted to live. He rode hard back toward the ranch house, telling himself that he was riding for help, but knowing that any help he might get would be too late to do any good.

He heard the shots behind him as he raced away, and then he felt one bite into his shoulder. He flinched, but he kept riding. He could feel the warm blood running down his chest and his back. He felt no pain, but he felt light-headed. He had to make it to the ranch house. He kicked his horse and lashed at it viciously.

Behind him, the pursuit stopped, Hank yelling out, "Let him go. Let's get back to the herd." The raiders turned their horses and rode back to where Guy and the others were still shooting the bawling animals. In a panic, the herd started to run, and both groups of raiders rode after them shooting and killing. At last they stopped. A few head of cattle had escaped the slaughter. "Come on," said Hank. "Let's get the hell outta here."

Slim weakened, and he stopped kicking and lashing, and the horse slowed down to a walk. Slim sagged in the saddle. He felt like he was going to sleep. He kept telling himself that he had to keep going. He had to get back to the ranch house and tell the boss what had happened out there. He could not afford to let himself drift into sleep. He talked to his horse, trying to keep awake. At last, he was overcome. He slipped into total darkness and fell out of the saddle. The horse kept going.

Slocum went to the corral early the next morning to saddle his big Appaloosa, and he found a brown horse, saddled and standing outside the corral gate. He looked around, but he saw no rider. He walked over to the horse, and he could see right away that it had suffered a hard ride. He decided to unsaddle it and worry about the details later, but when he walked around to begin the work, he saw the blood on the saddle. "Damn," he said.

He took the animal by the reins and started walking toward the big house. About halfway over, he could see that old Townsend had already stepped out onto the porch. As he moved closer, Townsend saw him and called out to him. "Slocum." Slocum walked on over to the porch.

"I just now found him standing by the gate outside the corral," Slocum said.

"Outside?"

"Yes, sir, and that ain't all."

He wiped his hand on the saddle and held it up for Townsend to see.

"Blood?"

"It's blood," said Slocum. "Whose horse is this?"

"It's mine," said Townsend. "I don't know who was riding it."

"Well, we better find out," said Slocum.

"Shotgun will know. I'll go get him."

"I'll take care of this poor horse," said Slocum.

Slocum led the horse back to the corral and pulled the saddle off its back. He tossed the saddle up on the top rail of the corral fence. Then he started back toward the house, but he saw Townsend coming with Shotgun. He walked to meet them.

"Slocum," said Townsend. "It was Slim riding that horse. He was out on the north pasture last night along with Hoss."

"Any sign of Hoss?" Slocum asked.

"No," said Shotgun.

"Well, there ain't no other stray horse," said Slocum.

"Let's get saddled up," said Townsend.

"Judging from that saddle," said Slocum, "we'd best have someone follow along with a wagon."

6

It wasn't long before they came across Slim, lying where he had fallen. He was bloody, and he was unconscious, but he was alive. They did what they could for him right there on the spot, and waited for the wagon to come along. When it arrived, they loaded poor Slim in the back and sent the driver with it back to the ranch house. Townsend told Shotgun to ride to town for the doc. That left just Old Man Townsend and Slocum on the range. They rode on to where Slim and Hoss had been assigned to ride herd the night before.

They were prepared for almost anything except what they found. The slaughtered cattle horrified them both. It was senseless killing. They were still stunned from the sight when they at last came across the body of Hoss. His dead horse was not far from where he lay.

"The dirty bastards," Townsend said.

"This is about as low a thing as I've ever seen," said Slocum.

"I never thought that Bob Amos would sink this low."

"Bob Amos?"

"He owns and runs the White Hat," Townsend said. "Me and him have never got along, but I sure never expected this from him. Well, he's declared war, and by God, he's going to get it."

"You mean to attack the White Hat?" Slocum asked.

"Hell, yes, I mean to."

"You got no proof of who done this here," said Slocum. "You got any law around here?"

"We got a sheriff, for what he's worth, and that ain't much."

"Let's talk to him at least."

"I know who's behind this, Slocum. I got no need to go to the sheriff."

"Maybe Slim will recover. Maybe he can tell us something."

"And maybe not. Why should I wait around for Amos to pull something else like this? How many cattle and how many men can I afford to lose while I wait?"

"I hate to go to killing someone without knowing for sure," Slocum said. "You do what you want. I'm going to town to see the sheriff."

"You're wasting your time, but I won't try to stop you."

It did not take Slocum long to find the sheriff's office in town. He hitched his horse to the rail in front and walked inside. A burly man in a sweat-stained white shirt looked up over a bushy mustache from behind a big desk cluttered with papers.

"Sheriff?" said Slocum.

"I'm Ace Corman, the sheriff."

Slocum walked over to stand by the desk. "I'm John Slocum. I work for Mr. Townsend. We had two boys shot last night along with a bunch of cattle. One of the boys is dead. The other one might not last."

"The cattle?"

"All killed."

"Now who the hell would want to go and do a thing like that?"

"Mr. Townsend says that it's the White Hat outfit," Slocum said. "Maybe he's right, but as far as I can tell, we got no proof. I told him I'd ride in and talk to you."

"Well, good," said Corman. "Good. You done the right thing, Slocum. Is Townsend fixing to ride against the White Hat?"

"I'm afraid that he is."

"Well, we'll have to try to stop him from doing that. We don't need no range war around here. Slocum. Say, ain't you the one that went and killed two White Hat boys in the saloon here?"

"I killed one of them," Slocum said. "He drew on me while my back was turned."

"Yeah. That's what all the witnesses said. That's how come I never went looking for you. Could be, though, that them two killings is what touched off that business last night."

"I reckon it likely is the reason," Slocum said, "but those two in the saloon were itching to start a fight, and they got it. Slim and Hoss were minding their own business. They were ambushed. Shot in cold blood. Hoss was murdered."

"Well, maybe. Let's take a ride out there and look things over. Wait for me out front while I go get a horse."

They walked outside, and Slocum took a cigar out of his pocket and lit it. He leaned back against the wall to wait for Corman's return. While he smoked and waited, Guy and Hank rode into town from the White Hat. They spotted him right away and rode straight to the rail next to the big Appaloosa. They sat in their saddles and stared at Slocum for a spell. Slocum puffed his cigar and stared back.

"You boys got a problem?" he said finally.

"What are you doing here at the sheriff's office?" asked Hank. "You got troubles?"

"We had some last night," Slocum said. "You two know anything about it?"

Both White Hat men laughed and looked at each other. "We don't know nothing," said Hank.

"I'll bet you don't. You either done it yourselves or else you know about it."

"Fuck you," said Guy.

"Why don't you stick around," said Slocum. "The sheriff'll be right back. Likely, he'll have some questions for you."

"If old Ace wants to talk to us, he knows where he can find us," said Hank. "Say, you're the son of a bitch that gunned down our pards in the saloon."

"Word does get around, don't it," said Slocum.

"Let's take him, Hank," said Guy.

Sheriff Ace Corman turned the corner on his black horse just in time to see the two White Hat men reach for their guns. He was astonished at the speed of Slocum, as he saw the gun flash in his hand and saw the two men jerk and fall from their saddles. He sat still for a moment, then urged his horse forward. Riding up to the scene, he dismounted.

"Trouble does seem to follow you around, Slocum," he said.

"I don't seem to have to go looking for it. They drew first."

"I seen it," said Corman. "You seem to have evened the score for last night. If Slim lives, you got one ahead on them."

"I ain't playing a game with those bastards, Sheriff," Slocum said.

"Yeah. Well, let me get the street cleaned off here, and we'll ride on out."

Across the street in the shadow of an overhanging roof, Stackpole watched. He watched as some men came to haul the bodies away, and he watched as Slocum and the sheriff mounted up to ride toward Townsend's place. He let them get out of town, and then he went to where his own horse waited. He mounted up and rode fast for the White Hat.

At the ranch, Slocum and Corman found Townsend organizing his crew for a raid. They shoved their way through the crowd of angry cowhands and walked up onto the porch to confront Townsend. Townsend scowled at Slocum. "So you brought the sheriff, did you?" the old man said. "Well, it ain't gonna do no good. Slim just died in there in my bed. Doc couldn't do nothing for him."

"Did he say anything before he died?" Slocum asked.

"He never had a chance."

"Then you still don't have any proof of who did the killing," said Slocum.

"I know."

"Townsend," said Corman, "hold on a bit. At least let me have my say."

"I'm listening," said Townsend.

Corman looked out over the crowd of armed cowboys. He looked back at Townsend. "Suppose you're right, but you never get any proof. You go killing a bunch of boys that works for ole Amos, and you even win the war. There'll have to be charges filed for all that killing, and without proof of what you're accusing them of, you'll be charged with murder."

He paused and looked out over the crowd. He thought he could see the expressions on their faces change a little.

"Well, what the hell am I supposed to do?" Townsend said.

"Let me do a little investigating," said Corman. "I'd like to ride out to the scene of the crime and have a look around."

"Me and Slocum done looked it over. Ain't nothing to be found there."

"I'd still like to look."

"Time's a-wasting," said Townsend.

"Just before we rode out here," said Corman, "two

White Hat men pulled down on Slocum in town. He killed them both."

Townsend looked at Slocum. "You killed two of them?"

"I did."

"Who were they? Do you know?"

"They was Hank and Guy," Corman said. "So in a way, you've done retaliated. Hold off for a spell on any more. Let me see what I can see."

"Killed Hank and Guy," Townsend mused. "I'll be damned."

Standing down at the front of the crowd, Cash smiled.

"You was the one wanting to hold off," Townsend said to Slocum.

"I didn't look for the fight," Slocum answered. "They pressed it."

"He's right, Mr. Townsend," said Corman.

"All right," said Townsend. "We'll hold off, but not for long."

"I'll ride out with you to where it happened," Slocum said.

"Let's go then," said Corman.

They walked down the stairs, and Cash stepped out in front of Slocum with a broad smile on his face. "The peacemaker, are you? Hell, pard, you've killed three of the bastards now."

Slocum pushed past Cash and mounted his big Appaloosa. He looked over to see if Corman was ready, then rode out with the sheriff just a little behind. Cash watched them go for a while. Then he walked up the steps to stand in front of Townsend.

"How long you gonna wait, boss?" he asked.

"Not long, Cash," said Townsend. "Not long."

Stackpole rode up to the main house on the White Hat, dismounted quickly, and rushed through the front door. Bob Amos looked up quickly. He relaxed when he saw that it was Stackpole. "You give up knocking, Stackpole?" he asked.

"Sorry, boss, but I just come from town. That gunfighter that old Townsend hired, that Slocum, he just killed Guy and Hank."

"In town? Both of them?"

"Right in front of the sheriff's office. The sheriff seen it too."

"Did he arrest Slocum?"

"Called it self-defense."

"Was it?"

"Well, I reckon it was. Really. I mean, Guy and Hank went for their guns first. But Slocum's fast, boss. Really fast."

"So he killed Guy and Hank. Damn."

"And boss, Slocum and the sheriff rode out of town together just ahead of me."

"They rode out together?"

"That's right. My guess is that Slocum went to see him about what happened out there last night, and he's going to investigate."

"Well, there won't be anything for him to find out, will there? Townsend will say that we done it, but all I have to do is deny it. There's no proof."

"The sheriff might hold Townsend off for a little while, but he'll be coming."

"Sure he will, and we'll be ready for him when he comes."

Slocum and Corman looked over the ground carefully, more carefully than had Slocum and Townsend. They found where the two separate groups had attacked, and they found plenty of shells, mostly forty-fives.

"They'll go in a Colt or a Winchester," said Slocum. "That ain't much help."

"Let's try to follow those tracks," Corman said.

They followed them for a while, and it looked like they

would lead over to the White Hat spread, but the tracks petered out before they led anywhere.

"What now?" Slocum asked.

"I mean to ride over and have a talk with Bob Amos," Corman said. "You want to come along?"

"I wouldn't mind meeting the man," said Slocum.

"All right. Let's go then."

Stackpole was keeping watch in front of the house. He opened the front door and peeked inside. "Here they come," he said.

Amos stood up and walked toward the door. "How many?"

"Just Ace Corman and Slocum."

"They just want to talk," said Amos. "You keep quiet. I'll handle it."

Amos stepped out of the house to stand beside Stackpole. He waited until the two riders had come close and halted their mounts. Then he said, "Howdy, Ace. What brings you out this way?"

"Two things," said Corman. "Couple of your boys got killed in town today."

"I heard," said Amos. He looked at Slocum. "Who done it?"

"I did," said Slocum. "They prodded me."

"Yeah," said Amos. "I heard that too."

"The other thing is, someone rode out to Townsend's north range last night and killed two cowboys and a whole bunch of cattle. The tracks we found looked like they come from here."

Amos looked at Stackpole. "Do you know anything about that?" he said.

"First I've heard of it," Stackpole said.

"Well, I'm sorry to hear it," Amos said to Corman, "but I can't help you any. Sorry you wasted your time riding all the way out here."

"Townsend thinks you done it, Amos, or had it done," Corman said.

"If Townsend fell off his horse, he'd blame me for it. You know that as well as I do. He's never liked me, and I don't know why. I mind my own business."

"You had four cowhands who liked to start fights," Slocum said.

"They're all dead now too, ain't they?" said Amos. "There shouldn't be any more trouble around here now."

"What about those tracks coming from your ranch?" asked Corman.

"You said they seemed to be coming from here," said Amos. "Which is it?"

"Well, they came from this direction, but they didn't really go all the way."

"I'd say they came from here," said Slocum.

Amos rubbed his chin. "Well," he said, "maybe they did. Come to think of it, them two you killed in town today was out last night. Do you know where they went, Stackpole?"

"You mean Guy and Hank? All I know is they said they was going into town to do some drinking. They was pretty well armed, though. I seen them when they left. It was just before dark."

"Maybe they done it, Sheriff," said Amos. "But if they did, they was on their own. I never give no order like that."

"It's awful handy, ain't it?" asked Slocum.

"What's that?" asked Amos.

"Accusing the dead."

7

At the main gate onto Townsend's ranch, Slocum and Corman stopped their horses. They sat for a moment without speaking, and then Corman said, "I'll just be heading on back into town, Slocum. I'm sorry, but tell ole Townsend there don't seem to be a thing I can do. My hands are tied. Now, if you could catch one of them doing something—"

"Like killing someone?" asked Slocum.

"Yeah. I'm sorry."

The sheriff turned his horse and went toward town. Slocum sat and watched him go for a while. Then he turned his Appaloosa onto the main road into the ranch. Along the way, he thought about the law. Oh, he believed in it all right, but usually, it seemed that out West the law was useless. A man had to stand up and fight for what was right or get run over. And it seemed like Townsend was in that position right now. Well, he wouldn't get any more arguments from Slocum. Slocum had gone to the law. He had gone through the motions. Now the law knew what was going on, and it had stepped aside. Its hands were tied, it had said. Wasn't that the same as to say handle it yourself? Well, Slocum took it that way.

Riding along, he tried to think of what would be the

next best move. He knew that Townsend had the men primed for an all-out attack on the White Hat, but he wasn't sure that was the best way. It might be best to just get ready for an attack, lay an ambush. If the fighting, the killing, was all done on Townsend's property, then it would be that much more obvious who was to blame. Maybe he would make that suggestion to ole Townsend when he got back.

He found Townsend sitting alone on the porch of his big ranch house, and he rode up to the porch and dismounted. He walked up the steps and stood looking at Townsend.

"I see the boys broke it up," Slocum said.

"They're ready to ride soon as I give the word," Townsend said.

"Sheriff says his hands are tied. There's no proof."

"I could a told you he'd say that."

"We rode over to the White Hat. That Bob Amos said he had nothing to do with it. Said maybe the two I killed in town did it on their own."

"Yeah?" said Townsend. "I could a told you that too. You wasted your time, Slocum."

"Well, Mr. Townsend, I don't think so. I think that now Corman knows what's going on, and when we do something, he'll just kind of look the other way. I don't think it was a waste of time."

"Maybe you're right. Well, are you with me then?"

"I'm with you. I have been all along."

"Then we'll attack those sonsabitches at sunrise. You can tell the boys."

"I'll tell them," Slocum said, his alternate plan gone out of his head. He turned to go down the steps, but the voice of Julie Townsend from the front door stopped him.

"Tell them what?"

Slocum turned. He took the hat off his head.

"That we're gonna attack the White Hat first thing in the morning," Townsend said.

"I see," said Julie.

"The sheriff said there was nothing he could do, ma'am," Slocum said. "I gave it a try. I rode out to the scene and then over to the White Hat with him. When we left, he said his hands were tied."

"Well," said Townsend, "mine ain't."

"But are you sure about this attack?" Julie asked.

"It seems like the only thing left to do," said Slocum.

"I see," Julie said. "Well, all right then."

"Good night, ma'am," said Slocum.

"Good night."

"I'll tell the boys, Mr. Townsend."

Slocum went down off the porch, mounted his Appaloosa, and rode over to the corral. There, he unsaddled his horse and turned it loose. He walked on to the bunkhouse. Inside, he found most of the hands. Cash and Monkey were seated on the edge of a bunk studying a Colt revolver. When Slocum stepped in the door, all talk stopped. Everyone looked at him.

"The boss says we go first thing in the morning," he said. "Everyone be ready."

He headed for his own bunk, and Cash got up and followed him. Monkey tagged along. "So we're going after them in the morning," Cash said.

"That's what the old man says," said Slocum.

"You going?"

"How come you ask me that?"

"Well, you didn't seem so hot on the idea earlier."

"I thought the sheriff ought to be told. Well, I told him. He ain't going to do anything. It's up to us."

"I see," said Cash. "I didn't think you was yellow."

Slocum looked hard into Cash's face, but he made no response.

"Well, it's late," Cash said. "I reckon we ought to turn in. We got early morning killing to do."

"Yeah," said Monkey nervously. "Good night, Slocum."
"Sleep well, boy," Slocum said.

The morning came early, but everyone was up and dress-
ing, checking weapons at the last minute. The cookshack
served up an early breakfast, and everyone ate hearty. For
some, it could be a last meal. Then they all went to the corral to saddle horses. Soon they were all mounted and ready
to go, waiting in front of the ranch house. A saddled horse
stood waiting at the porch. In another minute, Townsend
came out with a rifle in his hand. He stepped down off the
porch, shoved the rifle into the scabbard at the side of the
horse, and mounted up. Then he shouted over his shoulder
as he turned his horse, "Let's go, boys."

Slocum rode at Townsend's right, and Cash rode at his
left. Monkey rode to Cash's left. Shotgun Stone rode on
Slocum's other side. The rest of the boys came on behind.
It was still dark when they rode under the White Hat sign at
the main gate. The sun was just beginning to light up the
horizon in the east as they topped the slight rise off to the
front of the ranch house. There was no sign of life down
there. Townsend held up a hand to halt the march.

Cash glanced over at Monkey. "Ever shot at a man, kid?"
"No," Monkey said. "I ain't."
"It's not hard. Just think of them as targets, and you'll
do all right."

"Boys," said Townsend, "it looks like they're all still
asleep down there. We'll ride in as close as we can get.
Don't shoot till I do, unless someone spots us and starts
shooting first. When we do start shooting, make all the noise
you can. We don't want to give them time to wake up."

The old man cranked a shell into the chamber of his Winchester and started riding. The others moved right along
with him, some chambering shells in rifles, others pulling
six-guns out of holsters. They rode slowly at first. Then
Townsend picked up the pace. By the time they were within

shooting range of the ranch house and bunkhouse, they were riding fast. Townsend fired a shot through the front window of the ranch house, and then everyone started shooting. Any semblance of organization faded away as riders circled the ranch house and others raced for the bunkhouse. There was nothing really to shoot at, so they shot out windows.

Soon, however, shots were returned from both houses. One cowboy dropped off his horse. Some kept riding and shooting. Others dismounted to seek cover and continue the fight. One foolish White Hat hand came running out of the bunkhouse and was dropped immediately by several bullets. Gradually, the shooting slowed down. Men were picking their targets more carefully. Now there were men at the windows shooting back at them, and the men outside were trying to hit the men at the windows.

Cash and Monkey were down behind a wagon in front of the ranch house. Monkey fired again and again into the windows and the front wall of the house.

"Hey, kid," said Cash, "slow it down. Pick your targets now. Look at that window to the right of the front door. Watch it, and wait for that bastard to show himself. Then shoot."

Monkey sat still, his heart pounding. Then the man popped up and leveled a rifle out the window. Monkey fired, and the man dropped. Monkey looked at Cash with astonishment on his face. Cash grinned.

"See?" he said. "What'd I tell you. That's the way to do it."

Back at Townsend's ranch house, Julie paced the floor. She wondered what was happening. She worried about her uncle. She worried about all the boys. She was glad that they had Slocum and Cash on their side. They were real gunfighters. She had known that about them from the beginning. But then, Bob Amos had several such men in his employ. It was true that when Slocum and Cash had faced any of them, the two gunfighters had come out ahead. So far. She prayed that things would continue to go that way.

She fixed herself a cup of coffee and drank it, and then she began to pace some more. She looked at the clock. Then she walked out onto the porch and saw that the sun was high in the sky. She didn't think that she could take much more of this waiting. She walked off the porch and headed for the cookshack. Old Snaggletooth would be there. He was the only other one on the ranch who had stayed behind. She found Snaggletooth washing dishes.

"Here," she said. "Let me help you with that."

"Oh, no, ma'am," said Snaggletooth. "It's all part of my job. I can manage all right."

"I want to, Snaggletooth," she said. "I'm about to go crazy waiting for Uncle and the boys to get back. I've got to do something."

"Well, all right, ma'am," Snaggletooth said. "If you put it that way. I got to peel some taters."

Snaggletooth moved over to a table with a stack of potatoes on it and took up a knife. He started whittling on a big potato. Julie was scrubbing dishes and had her back to Snaggletooth.

"I wouldn't worry too much, ma'am," Snaggletooth said. "Your uncle is a tough old man. He's come through plenty a fights in his time. He'll come through this one."

"I'm sure you're right, Snaggletooth. It's just the waiting around. Sometimes I wish I were a man."

"Oh, I wouldn't be wishing that," said Snaggletooth. "You're a fine woman. Just you wait. They'll be riding back in here soon."

"Pass the word around, Slocum," said Townsend. "Let's go, but don't leave anyone behind."

"All right," said Slocum, and he hollered out the order from where he crouched. Then he ran to call it out again. At last, he jumped on the back of his Appaloosa and began to ride around the main house, spreading the word. He rode around the bunkhouse the same way. At last, he rode up to the body lying on the ground, and he picked it up and threw it across his saddle. Then he remounted. A shot whizzed past his ear, and he turned and snapped off a shot at the nearest window.

In a short while, the entire Townsend crew was back on the road, riding toward home. As far as Slocum knew, he had the only body that needed to be brought back. He knew that there were several wounded. A couple of them had to be helped. He also knew that the Amos side had suffered more casualties than had Townsend's. Monkey rode up beside Slocum.

"How come you called us off?" he said. "We didn't get them all."

"They had enough," said Slocum.

"We shouldn't a stopped till we'd killed them all," Monkey shouted.

"They were my orders," said old Townsend.

Monkey shut up and dropped back to ride along in silence beside Cash. Cash let him go on like that for a while. At last he said, "Hey, kid, there'll be other times."

"I just don't see why we didn't finish it when we had the chance."

"We were running low on ammunition, and we got wounded. Two good reasons to quit while you're ahead. Don't worry."

Slocum was worried, though. He was worried about what Cash was making of the kid. He was afraid that if something did not slow Monkey down, and real soon, the kid would be in for a short life. He might make a good gunfighter, given time, but he was not exhibiting the kind of patience required for that to happen. He was a good enough kid too. He was just too taken with Cash. That was all.

When they rode into the yard in front of the house, Shotgun was sent to town for the doc. In the meantime,

Julie, Snaggletooth, and Slocum were busy with the wounded. They patched them up as best they could. Snaggletooth made a big pot of coffee, and when they had done all they could for the wounded, they sat and drank coffee. The day was only half gone, yet Slocum felt like he had put in a full day of work.

The doc showed up to patch the wounds, and because he had to unwrap them to check them, he also had to rewrap them. He declared, though, that he hadn't really been needed. A good job had been done in the first place. He packed his bag up and left to go back to town. At last, Townsend, Slocum, Julie, Cash, and Monkey were sitting on the porch. Townsend and Slocum smoked big cigars. They had coffee all around.

"Monkey," said Townsend, "I want to explain something to you."

"Oh, you don't need to explain nothing to me, Mr. Townsend. You're the boss. What you say goes. I shouldn't a spoke up the way I did."

Slocum raised his eyebrows. He was pleased. Maybe there was hope for the kid yet.

"I called off the fight because I knew that we had men hurt. We lost one killed, and that's a shame. I didn't want more men hurt or killed. The purpose of this morning's raid was to serve notice to Amos. If he wants a war, we're ready to give him one. Well, he's got that message now. If he's willing to call it off now, that'll be all right with me. I figure we've evened the score with him. But if he wants to keep it up, well, we're ready and willing, and he knows that now."

"Yes, sir," said Monkey. "I understand. It's just that—"

"It's just that you were still hot from the battle," said Townsend. "I know the feeling, and I appreciate it. You showed yourself good this morning, young man. I'm proud to have you with me."

"Thanks," said Monkey.

"Now, Slocum, Cash, what do you two think we ought to do next? Maybe I should ask, if you was in Amos's shoes, what would you be doing?"

"I'd be gathering my forces to strike back," said Cash.

"How soon?" asked Townsend.

"I'd say right now," Slocum said.

"Right now?" asked Julie. "So soon?"

"That's how he'll be hoping we'll think," Slocum said. "We've just been through the same fight as him. We got men hurt. We ain't ready for another fight just yet. What better time for him to hit us?"

"But can he pull together fast enough?" asked Townsend.

"That's the question," said Cash, "but if he can, Slocum's right. He'll be coming."

8

They made hasty plans. According to old Townsend, there were only three practical approaches onto his property from the direction of the White Hat. They decided to place lookouts at each of those locations. Two men would watch, and if they were to see anyone coming, one would stay, while the other rode as fast as he could back to the ranch house to warn the others. The whole force of cowhands would not go out at once, however, in case there was some kind of trick, such as attacking with a divided force from two different directions at the same time. The rest of the men were to remain ready to go at a moment's notice. They were to be armed, weapons ready, horses saddled.

Slocum, Cash, and Monkey stayed at the ranch house on the porch, waiting for any word from any of the lookouts. The air was tense. Cash and Monkey talked about guns and their use. Slocum lit a cigar. Old Man Townsend came out of the house to sit with them, and just after him, Julie brought out a tray of coffee and cups and passed the coffee around. She put the tray on a table and sat down on the porch with the men.

"Mr. Slocum?" she asked.

"I'd appreciate it if you'd drop the mister, ma'am," said Slocum.

"I'll do that if you'll drop the ma'am. My name's Julie."

Slocum smiled. "All right, Julie," he said. "What is it?"

"What do you mean?"

"You were about to say something to me."

"Oh, yes," she said, blushing slightly. "I was just going to ask you if you really believe they'll attack us right away."

"I only believe that they'll attack us. It could be right away, and it could be several days from now. We got to stay ready, whenever it comes."

"I see. How strong do you think they are? I mean, how are we matched?"

"Judging from what I've seen so far, I'd say we're about even. We could be in for a long war, if that's what you're asking me."

"Yes," she said. "I was afraid of that."

"I ain't sure either, ma'am—uh, Julie, how bad we hurt them this morning. That'll have a lot to do with how quick they come back at us."

"Well, we'll be ready for them," said Townsend. "They're going to get more fight than they ever counted on."

"That's for sure," said Monkey. "We'll wipe them out."

A rider came fast toward the porch, coming in from the north. As he came in close enough, he shouted, "They're coming down the north pass."

Everyone jumped to their feet. Townsend called out to the rider, "Change your horse and get back out there."

"Yes, sir."

"Let's go, men," said Townsend.

"Hold on, boss," said Slocum. "We can't all of us go on this one. Remember our plans. What if they split their force? Someone has to be here to go with the second crew."

"Slocum's right," said Cash. "You and Slocum stay here. Me and Monkey will go out with this first bunch."

"But I—"

Slocum shrugged and sat back down. "Guess we'll sit this one out, Mr. Townsend. I haven't finished my coffee anyhow."

"Damn it to hell," Townsend grumbled as he sat back down. Cash and Monkey hurried for their horses. Other hands came out from the bunkhouse, and soon about half of the ranch crew was headed out for the north pass ready to fight. Cash rode in the lead. Monkey rode beside him. Shotgun Stone was right there with them.

"Don't worry about them, Mr. Townsend," Slocum said. "I've never known an abler man than that Cash. The rest of your crew is good too. He'll lead them through this okay."

The north pass was just what its name implied. It was a narrow pass between steep hills on both sides. The look-outs had been posted high with spyglasses so that they could get word back to the ranch house in time to get men back to the pass once any attackers had been spotted. Cash and his crew arrived in time. They got up into the hills on both sides of the pass. Cash had given his instructions that no one was to fire until he did. The White Hat riders were getting close.

Cash waited, perched behind a boulder, his Henry rifle ready. The riders came closer. Still, he waited. Then, when the White Hat crew was almost directly below them, he fired. His whole crew began firing. Three White Hat hands dropped from their horses. Others dismounted and quickly ran for cover. A few fired from horseback, but they were soon picked off by the men on the hill-sides. From his perch, Monkey was thrilled. He had already knocked three men out of their saddles. His score was now four men killed. The blood raced through his veins.

From Cash's location, he could see Monkey, and though he was busy with his own killing, he managed to watch the young man, and he smiled at what he saw. The kid was doing all right for himself. Two of Townsend's men were hit, but the battle was one-sided. The White Hat men down below began watching for chances to get back on their mounts and get away. A couple of them were killed in the attempt. Several escaped. At last the fight was over. Cash stood up and called for a cease-fire. There was no one left below to shoot at.

"They're coming through the front gate," shouted the rider approaching the house.

Slocum, Townsend, and others mounted up quickly and headed for the front gate. They arrived at their ambush spot in the nick of time. Earlier preparations had placed wagons and bales of hay on both sides of the road. Everything around was flat. The riders dismounted and hid behind the makeshift barrier as quickly as they could. Slocum was to Townsend's right behind the stacks of hay. In another moment, the White Hat riders came barreling down the road. The Townsend outfit waited until they were close enough for the shots to count. Then they opened fire.

Several White Hat riders fell at the first volley. It was an unfair situation. The White Hat riders had no cover. They fired back for a few moments. Then they turned and fled the scene. Slocum stood up and watched them go.

"That was too easy, Slocum," Townsend said.

"We caught them by surprise," said Slocum. "Next time could be way different."

"I can't see how," Townsend said. "We hit them hard this morning. Now, when they come back at us, we hit them hard again."

"They'll be more careful next time," Slocum said. "And we don't know yet how Cash and them made out."

They left a couple of lookouts to guard the way again, and the bulk of the crew went back to the ranch house. When they got there, Cash and Monkey were already sitting on the porch. Julie was serving coffee again. Slocum took his Appaloosa and Townsend's mount and put them away. Then he returned to the porch to join the others there. When he sat down, Julie said, "Coffee?"

"Yes," he said. "Thank you."

She served him a cup and then sat down facing him.

"Uncle says you drove them off without a single loss," she said.

"We did," said Slocum. He looked over at Cash. "How'd you boys do?"

"Two wounded," Cash said. "None killed."

"And the other side?"

"Hell, I lost count. We peppered them good. You should a seen the kid here. He got at least three of them. Or was it more than that, kid?"

Monkey looked down at the boards in the porch, showing modesty and a little embarrassment, but also a tremendous amount of pride. "No, Cash," he said, "it was just them three. That's all."

"Hell, kid, I only knocked four of them down myself. You're doing real good. You're going to be first-rate. I can tell you that right now."

"Thanks, Cash."

"How many did you get, Slocum?" Cash asked.

"I don't know," Slocum said. "I don't keep count of such things."

"Well, you oughta, Slocum," said Monkey. "I mean, how else you going to build up your reputation?"

"Kid," said Slocum, "I generally don't give lectures, so I'm just going to say this to you one time. The only thing a reputation like that is good for is to get you killed while you're still young. The more men that you're known to have killed, the more men will come around gunning for you. One of them's going to get you one of these days."

Cash sipped the last of his coffee and put down the cup. He slapped Monkey on the shoulder and said, "Come on, kid."

The two men left the porch and walked toward the bunkhouse. Julie broke the uneasy silence by standing up to get the coffeepot. "Refill, Slocum?"

"Thanks," he said.

"That was an unusual lecture you gave Monkey," she said. "It's not what one would expect from a gunfighter."

"I don't call myself a gunfighter, Julie. If you recall, I came here to work as a cowhand. That's all."

"But when trouble started," she said, "you were right out in front."

"I don't look for trouble, but when it finds me, I don't run from it either."

"I'm not criticizing you," she said. "I'm glad you're here, and I'm glad that you're on our side. I just can't quite figure you out. That's all."

"I been trying to do that for myself for most of my life."

"I'm just glad to have you and Cash with me," said Townsend. "And young Monkey. Cash's bringing him along right well. And right now, we need all the gunfighting help we can get."

Slocum sipped his coffee. He had several things he wanted to say, but he decided that they were best left unsaid. He finished what he had in the cup and set it down. Standing, he said, "I don't think we'll be hit again today. I'm going on over to the bunkhouse and try to get some sleep."

He touched the brim of his hat and left the porch. Walking slowly, he went past the corral and on over to the bunkhouse. Inside, he found Cash and Monkey sitting together on the edge of a bunk. Monkey was cutting notches into the handle of his six-gun. Slocum gave him a disapproving look as he walked by on the way to his own bunk. He took off his gun belt and hung it on the wall beside his bunk. Then, he sat down and pulled off his boots. Lying back, he tilted his hat to cover his face, and soon he was asleep.

Monkey finished his carving and held the gun out to

look at it. He looked up at Cash with pride in his expression. "How's that?"

"Looks good, kid," Cash said. "Hey, let's get out of here."

"Where we going, Cash?"

"To town, boy. Whiskey and women."

"All right."

They saddled their horses, and were in town at the saloon in a short while. They sauntered inside and bellied up to the bar. "Whiskey," Cash called out. The barkeep poured them a couple of shots, and Cash took hold of the bottle. "Leave it," he said.

"Wonder where Honey Pot is at," said Monkey.

"It's a little early in the day," said Cash, "but she'll be around. Don't worry, kid."

"Aw, I ain't worried. Hell. We got us a good bottle of whiskey here, ain't we?"

"Yeah. You're catching on."

The doors swung open, and two cowboys walked in. Cash punched Monkey on the shoulder. In a low voice, he said, "See that?"

"What?" asked Monkey. "Them two that just came in?"

"Yeah."

"What about them?"

"They're White Hatters, boy."

"Oh?"

"Yeah. Be ready for trouble, kid."

"I'm always ready. They want any trouble, I'm right here."

He said that last in a loud enough voice to be heard. The two White Hat men turned to face Monkey and Cash. They walked slowly toward them. Drawing closer, one of them took note of the freshly carved notches on Monkey's six-gun handle.

"Hey, you," he said.

Monkey turned to face the men. "You talking to me?"

"Them notches all come from shooting White Hat men from ambush?"

"I got room for two more," said Monkey.

"You think you can take the two of us?"

Cash stepped out to stand beside Monkey. "It's two against two," he said. "Make your play."

"Keep out of this, Cash," Monkey said. "He asked me can I take the two of them. Well, I can."

"You sure, kid?"

"Stay out of it."

Cash held his hands up and backed away. "Have it your way. I'm out of it. Unless they kill you. Then I'll take my turn."

"That's fair enough. Well, you two. You gonna make a play or stand there with your thumbs up your asses?"

Both White Hat men went for their guns at once, but the kid was fast. His first shot shattered the sternum of the man on the right. His second tore into the other's shoulder. The first man dropped to the floor. The second yelled out in pain and anger and raised his revolver. The kid fired a third shot, which struck the man in the forehead. He stood there for a moment, marveling at his own work, not quite believing what he had done or what he had become. Casually, he ejected the empty shells from the chambers of his Colt, and he reloaded. Then he put the six-gun away. Cash stepped up to him and threw an arm around his shoulders.

"Kid, that was fast. As fast as I've seen. You took them both, and you took them fair. They drew first. Both of them." He looked around the room. "You all seen it, didn't you?"

"We did," said a man at a table. "It was self-defense all right."

Several other voices joined his in defending Monkey. In another minute, Sheriff Corman came into the saloon, but all who were present backed up Monkey. "I'll just get someone to clean up," Corman said.

Cash poured out two more drinks, and the kid drank his down in a hurry and poured again. "Kid," said Cash, "you got two more notches to carve now."

"Yeah," said Monkey.

"And kid, these two are different. These two are for men you took out fair, while they was facing you. There won't be any question now. You've become a top gun, kid. A real gunfighter."

9

Several days passed without much happening, and Slocum went back to working as a cowhand. He hoped that the war was over. He wasn't damn fool enough to quite believe it, though. He stayed alert, and old Townsend did keep the lookouts posted. Slocum could tell that Cash and Monkey were getting restless. They were longing for more action. Neither of them had chosen to go back to cowboy work. They were happy being paid as gunfighters. Slocum tried to put them out of his mind, but he was worried about young Monkey.

While Slocum was riding the range, Cash and Monkey passed the hours checking at the various lookout stations, practicing with their weapons, or drinking and looking for fights in town. One quiet afternoon, Cash proposed to Monkey that they take a ride.

"Where we going, Cash?" Monkey asked.

"Just come along with me," Cash said.

They rode out of the Townsend ranch and onto the road. Monkey thought that they would be going to town, and that was all right with him. However, it soon became apparent that they were heading elsewhere.

"Hey, Cash, are we going to the White Hat?"

"You figured it, kid."

"We gonna shoot the place up some?"

"Not today. I got something else in mind."

"Well," Monkey said, "you gonna tell me about it?"

"The White Hat ain't come back at us, have they?"

"No."

"I think we hit them bad. I don't think they can come back at us."

"You mean we whipped them?"

"Damn near. But I think if they had a chance to hire on a couple or three good gunslingers, they'd jump at it, and they'd pay better'n ole Townsend too, on account a they're desperate. You follow me?"

"You mean—us?"

"Sure. Slocum too, if he's a mind."

"He won't be."

"Well, that's his problem. What do you say, kid?"

"Quit ole Townsend and go to work for the White Hat," Monkey mused.

"There ain't nothing happening right now, is there? And the money'd be better."

"How do we know the money'd be better?"

"Well, if it ain't, we don't do it. So what do you say?"

"We might have to face down Slocum, Cash."

"Does that worry you, kid?"

"It don't worry me, but I thought he was your pard."

"Hey, we rode together awhile, but you're my pard. Don't forget that."

"Well, hell, Cash, in that case, I'm with you. All the way. Let's ride on in there and talk to ole Amos."

They moved on, and when they came to the gateway to the White Hat, they found a guard there.

"Hold it," he said.

"We wanta talk with your boss," Cash said.

"I ain't sure about that," said the guard.

"You want to shoot it out?" asked Monkey.

"Well, there's just the two of you," said the guard. "Ride on in. I'll ride along with you."

At the ranch house, Bob Amos had heard the horses approaching. He stepped out the front door. He recognized Cash and Monkey immediately. "What do you want here?" he said.

"Don't get hostile, Amos. We didn't come to fight, and we didn't come to make no demands. We just come to have a little chat. That's all. Can we get down?"

"You got a lot of balls riding in here like this," Amos said. "I know you're fast, but you're way outnumbered. I could have you shot down easy."

"I could kill you before I dropped," said Monkey.

"Yeah, well, climb on down and talk," said Amos.

Cash swung down out of the saddle, and Monkey followed him. They hitched their horses to the rail in front of the ranch house, and Amos opened the front door. "Come on in," he said. They stepped into Amos's large front room, and he indicated some easy chairs. Cash and Monkey took seats. Amos got a box of cigars and passed it around. Each man took a cigar and lit it. Then Amos sat directly across from Cash. "Now," Amos said, "what's on your mind?"

"We've been waiting for a counterattack," said Cash. "None's come."

"You come here to gloat?" asked Amos. "I could have you killed easy enough."

"We done went over that," said Monkey. "Likely you'd go with us."

"Yeah. Well. You talk. I'm listening."

"It's been several days now, Amos," said Cash. "How come you ain't hit us back yet? Could it be you're short-handed? We killed too many of your men?"

"Say that was the case," said Amos. "What makes you think I'd tell you?"

"We ain't here to spy on you," Cash said. "Me and Monkey here, we're professional gunfighters. It's beginning to look like there ain't no more work for us around here. We're just wondering if we have to pull up stakes and move on."

"Has Townsend cut you loose?" asked Amos, his eyes opening wide.

"Well, he seems to think he's gone past our kind of work. Thinks there won't be no more need of gunfighters."

"What are you getting at?" asked Amos. "Are you getting at what I think you're getting at?"

"We're just a couple of gunfighters looking for action, Mr. Amos," said Cash. "That's all. Nothing very complicated."

"You'd change horses in the middle of the stream? You've killed a number of my men already."

"We kill for pay," said Cash.

"Nothing more," said Monkey.

"Well, I'll be damned. You want to come to work for me?"

"If the pay's good enough."

"What about that Slocum?"

"I figure we'll ask him if he wants to come along with us."

"I don't want him. I want you to kill him."

Monkey gave Cash a look, but Cash ignored it. "That would be most of the job right there," he said. "Without us two and Slocum, Townsend wouldn't have anything."

"I'll pay you a thousand dollars to kill Slocum," said Amos.

"A thousand apiece," Cash said.

Amos thought for a moment. "All right. All right. A thousand apiece. After you get rid of Slocum, we'll talk about more permanent arrangements."

Cash and Monkey were riding back toward the Townsend spread at a leisurely pace. They rode for a while in silence. At last, Monkey spoke up. "Cash," he said, "I thought Slocum was your friend."

"He helped me out of a jam once," said Cash, "but that don't make me his keeper."

"I don't get it."

"Kid, if you want to make a living with that six-gun of yours, you can't let sentimental thinking get in your way. Slocum's worth a thousand apiece to us right now. That's good pay. You ever seen a thousand dollars, kid?"

"No. I ain't. Never."

"Did you ever expect to?"

"No, I didn't. A thousand dollars."

"What do you think about Slocum now, kid?"

"Why, hell, Cash, I think I can take him."

"Now you're talking."

The lookout was still on duty at the main gate when Cash and Monkey rode back onto the Townsend spread. They hailed him as if nothing was wrong and rode on in. Cash had told Monkey to make like everything was just fine. Put on the pretense that they were still with Townsend. They would watch for their chance at Slocum, but likely it would not be there on the ranch. They would have to get him off by himself somewhere.

"Just play it cool, kid," Cash said. "We'll get our chance."

They got back to the corral at the same time Slocum was returning from the range. Together, they unsaddled and took care of their horses, turning them loose in the corral. Then they walked toward the cookshack.

"Have a rough day?" Cash asked.

"Not bad," said Slocum. "How much longer are you two going to lay around getting paid for nothing?"

"Hell, Slocum, we're being paid for looking out for this place against the White Hat. Why the hell should we bust our ass chasing cows? What the hell are you doing it for?"

"Seems like the fighting's over," Slocum said. "I'm just trying to give the man an honest day's work for my pay. That's all."

"Well, you just go on and do that. Me and Monkey here, we'll keep watching the trails to protect you cowhands from any danger."

Slocum gave Cash a look, but he did not bother responding to that remark. They found their places at the table and sat down to eat. Slocum ate enough for two men. It had been a rough day, but he would not admit that to Cash. A long day of chasing half-wild animals through rugged terrain. They were about done with their meal. Most of the men had gotten up and left. Slocum had one more cup of coffee, and Cash decided that he and Monkey would stay too.

"You really think the fighting's over and done?" Cash asked Slocum.

"We hit Amos hard three times," Slocum said. "That's not to mention the boys of his we got in town. If he had any strength left, he'd have come back at us by now. At least, that's the way it looks to me."

"Yeah? Well, maybe you're right about that. Maybe we should go back to being ordinary cowhands, like you done."

"What made you change your mind about that?"

"Oh, I've just been thinking about what you said. That's all. You know, about an honest day's work for the old man. I never was one to take no charity." Monkey was giving Cash a puzzled look, but he kept his mouth shut. "What do you say, kid? Shall we go back to work? Be honest cowhands like our ole pard here?"

Monkey gave a shrug. "Whatever you say, Cash."

Cash turned up his cup and drained it. Then he stood up. "Come on," he said. "Let's go talk to the boss."

Monkey got up to follow him. Slocum sat for a moment longer over his coffee, puzzling over Cash's behavior. Just what the hell was he up to? He was not that fond of hard work. Slocum had figured out that much about the man some time ago. He was a good man to have on your side during a fight, but beyond that, he wasn't worth much of a shit. Slocum finished his coffee and got up to follow those two over to the ranch house.

When he got there, he found them on the porch: Cash, Monkey, Townsend, and Julie.

"Come on up and join us, Slocum," said Townsend. "The boys here was telling me that they want to go back to work."

"Yeah?" Slocum stepped up onto the porch and took a chair. He took off his hat. "Evening, Julie," he said.

"Good evening," she said with a smile.

"Slocum," said Townsend, "do you think it's safe for these two to go back to work the way you done? Do you really think we've won this war with Amos?"

"Well, sir," said Slocum, "right now, it looks that way to me. We hurt him pretty bad, and he's not fighting back. He could go out recruiting some more hands, more gunfighters, but we don't know that he's been doing that. If we find out that he is, then we can go back to the way we been doing things."

"Well, that makes sense to me," said Townsend.

"Uncle," said Julie, "are you sure?"

"There won't be nothing to worry about, miss," said Cash, leering at Julie. "Slocum, me, and Monkey, we'll all still be right here on the ranch. We still got guards out, don't we? If anyone's coming, they can get word out to us fast enough."

"Then it's settled," Townsend said. "In the morning, you two ride on out with Slocum. He'll catch you up on where he's at and what's going on. Well, I'm going to turn in. It's been a long day."

Townsend got up and headed for the door, and the others all said good night to him. Slocum stood up. "We ought to be turning in too," he said. "Good night."

"Good night," said Julie.

Slocum walked down off the porch. He looked back at Monkey and Cash.

"Go on, kid," said Cash. "I'll be along."

Monkey joined Slocum walking back to the bunkhouse. Julie started to stand up.

"You don't need to be in a hurry," said Cash, "do you?"

"Well, no," she said. "I guess not. Do you have something on your mind?" Cash looked at her, and it became suddenly obvious what was on his mind. Julie got nervous. She stood up. "It has been a long day, Mr. Cash. I'll say good night."

Cash stood quickly and grabbed her by an arm. "Don't rush off," he said. "We got a lot to talk about."

"We have nothing to talk about," she said.

"Maybe you're right. Talking's a waste of time." He took hold of her by both her shoulders and pulled her toward him, bending his head to try to force a kiss. Julie twisted her face away from him.

"Stop it," she said. "Let me go."

Cash slipped one arm around behind her back. He pulled her close to him. She put both hands on his chest in an attempt to push him away. Cash's other hand went behind her head and his fist closed on a handful of hair. Still, she twisted her face, but Cash pressed against her. He managed to get his lips on hers, and while she clamped her mouth tight and continued to struggle, he slobbered a wet kiss over her mouth and face.

Julie slipped one hand loose and pulled Cash's head away from her by his hair. With her other hand, she slapped him hard across the face. Surprised, he turned loose of her, and she stepped back, glaring at him.

"Get out of here," she said. "Stay away from me."

"Ain't that the way you like it?" he said, rubbing his face where she had slapped him.

"Not like that," she said, "and not any other way from you."

"I suppose you'll go tell Uncle about this and get me fired," Cash said.

"No," she said. "I won't do that. But if you ever touch me again, I'll kill you."

She turned and went into the house, slamming the door behind her. Cash stood on the porch and laughed.

10

The next day passed without incident. Cash and Monkey rode out with Slocum, and they did their share of the work. Slocum was uneasy with them, however. Trying not to be too obvious about it, he kept his eye on them. He kept them in front of him. Now and then, one or both of them got behind him, but as quickly as was possible without giving himself away, he changed his position. They made small talk, the way men will do when they work together.

Slocum had dismounted to untangle his rope following a bout with an ornery cow, and he was not paying too much attention to the other two. Out of the corner of his eye, he saw Monkey pull out his six-gun. Quickly, he went for his own, but he had it only halfway up when the blast from Monkey's revolver made his ears ring. The shot had come close to him, but it did not hit him. Slocum sensed that something was wrong. He held his own gun, not quite up and pointed at Monkey, while Monkey reholstered his. Slocum looked down to see a dead rattler not far from his feet. He put away his own gun.

"Thanks, Monkey," he said.

"If you were any faster," said Monkey, "you might've killed me."

"Yeah," said Slocum. "Sorry about that. It was just a reflex action."

Slocum went back to his work, and Monkey rode over to Cash, out of earshot of Slocum. "Good shooting, kid," said Cash.

"Not bad, I guess."

"You could've taken him, you know."

"I beat him all right," Monkey said, "but I drawed first."

"Even so, he wouldn't have come close. You can take him, kid. You can take him."

"You want me to do it?"

"Not now, and not here. We'll wait a bit."

It was Friday evening, and Slocum volunteered to take the place of the lookout who was watching the front entrance. Most of the boys would be going into town, and Slocum figured that if he went, he would just sit and drink with Cash and Monkey. He was not in the mood for that. The man he freed from duty was very appreciative, and Slocum was content. He waved at the boys as they rode past him on their way to town. Among them were Shotgun Stone, Cash, and Monkey.

"We'll drink a few for you," said Cash as he rode by.

Slocum leaned back on the stack of hay bales after the riders had all gone their way. He thought about Cash and Monkey. He wondered if he should have left well enough alone when he first set eyes on Joe Cash. He wondered if he should have let him hang. He'd seemed all right for a time, but then he had gotten a hold on young Monkey, and Slocum did not like what he was seeing happen to the kid.

While he was thus musing, he heard the sound of another horse approaching from behind him. Looking over his shoulder, he saw Julie riding toward him. He stood up, took off his hat, and waited for her approach. She stopped her horse beside his Appaloosa and dismounted.

"Howdy, Julie," he said. "What brings you out this way? Not headed for town, are you?"

"I came out to see you," she said. "Brought some sandwiches and coffee. You interested?"

"I sure am, and thanks."

She settled down beside him against the hay bales, and took out the stuff she had in a basket. Slocum ate a sandwich. Then he sat back to sip a cup of coffee. He could still watch the road from his position. "That was mighty good, Julie. I appreciate it. Do you do that for all the boys on watch?"

"You're my first," she said.

"How come me?"

"Oh, I don't know," she said. "Maybe I just like you."

"That's a dangerous thing for a lady to say."

"Because you'll just take what you can and then ride away?" asked Julie.

"Something like that."

"That's no big surprise. It shows in you. A woman would be a damn fool to expect to hold you for long."

"And that doesn't bother you?"

"No. It doesn't."

She put a hand on his shoulder and leaned in to give him a kiss. He responded, gently at first. Then he put both his arms around her and kissed her hard and passionately. Finally, they broke apart. Julie was panting for breath.

"I am on duty here, you know," Slocum said.

"You won't always be on duty," she said. "There'll be another time. Other times."

"Yeah. There will be. You don't have to go yet, though, do you?"

"Not just yet."

Slocum took her hand in his. "I'd like for you to stay. You're pleasant company for a lonely man."

In town, Monkey and Cash were getting drunk. Shotgun Stone was at the bar with a couple of other hands from

Townsend's ranch. Everyone seemed to be having a good time. As far as anyone knew, there were no White Hat hands in the place.

"I reckon they're scared to come in," Shotgun said to the men with him. "We've whipped them too many times."

"Hell, Shotgun," said one of the boys with him, "there may not be any left over there to come into town at all."

Shotgun laughed. "You might be right about that. This fight was damn near over before it begun."

"And I suppose it was all your doing, Shotgun," said Cash in a loud voice, intruding himself into the conversation.

Shotgun and the others got quiet. Shotgun turned to face Cash. "I never said that, Cash. 'Course, I done my part all right."

"I don't recall seeing you in the fight," Cash said. "You was back in the bunkhouse waiting for us to get the job done, wasn't you?"

"I was in it all right. I was right there."

"Bullshit."

"What the hell are you doing, Cash? You trying to provoke me into a fight? I don't want to fight you. Ain't no reason for it. We're all on the same side here."

"I don't see that it makes much difference what side you're on."

"Well," said Shotgun, turning his back on Cash, "I ain't gonna fight you. That's all."

"You're a chicken shit," said Cash.

"No, I ain't."

"I say you're a chicken shit, and you either agree with me or go for your gun."

"Let's get out of here, Shotgun," said the cowhand next to him.

"No, by God," Shotgun said, whirling and pulling out his revolver at the same time. Cash's was out before Shotgun could get his level, and it barked death. The slug tore into Shotgun's chest. He sagged against the bar, and then he sat

down heavily on the floor. He was dead. The cowhands
who had been with him picked up the body and left the
saloon. Cash put away his gun and sat back down.

"That's one less, kid," he said.

"You've give us away, though," Monkey said. "We can't
go back to Townsend's tonight after that."

"Sure we can. I didn't give nothing away about our new
situation with Amos. My fight with Shotgun was over the
way he acted during our gun battles. It was a personal fight.
That's all. We'll go back to Townsend's all right. Don't
worry about that."

"Well, hell," said Monkey with a shrug, "whatever you
say."

"I say let's have another drink."

"That's all right, pard," said Monkey, "but I'm thinking
about going upstairs with Honey Pot here in just a little bit."

Slocum was still on guard when the two boys came back to
the ranch with the body of Shotgun Stone. He heard them
approaching and stood up with his rifle. It was way too early
for any of the boys to be coming back, but as they drew
closer, he recognized them. Then he saw what they were
bringing along, slung across a third horse. Slocum thought
that he recognized the horse as the one Shotgun had ridden
to town, but he wasn't sure, or he did not want to be sure.

"Who've you got there?" he said.

"It's Shotgun, Slocum. Cash shot him dead in the saloon."

"Cash?"

"Picked a fight with him on purpose, he did. Shotgun said
he didn't want to fight, but Cash finally egged him into it."

"Who drew first?"

"Shotgun did."

"Damn," said Slocum.

"We best get him up to the ranch house and let the boss
know what happened."

"Yeah. Go on ahead. Damn it."

Slocum watched them ride on until they were out of his sight. Then he sat back down. He was still holding his rifle in his left hand. With his right, he shoved back the hat on his head. What the hell was Cash up to? Was he just bored with a few days of peace? Did he need a fight that bad? Why the hell did he have to kill Shotgun? He would say, of course, that it had been a fair fight, that Shotgun had pulled first and he had only defended himself. It was his pattern, and it would work, of course, with the law.

Slocum wondered, though, what Townsend would do. If Cash had the gall to come back out to Townsend's, would Townsend buy his story, just like the sheriff would, and let him stay on? And what was Monkey doing all the time Cash was starting a fight and killing Shotgun? Suddenly, Slocum wished that he would be relieved. He felt as if there were things he needed to be checking on. He needed to see Townsend, and he wanted to confront Cash.

There was nothing he could do, though. He was on duty. And he would likely still be on duty until everyone else was asleep. He guessed it would all have to wait till morning. He wondered, though, if he would be able to sleep. He wondered if anyone would. Anyone other than Cash and Monkey. They would sleep just fine, wherever they chose to bed down for the night.

Slocum stood up and paced for a few minutes. Then he mounted the Appaloosa and rode the trail from his post to the main gate and back again. At last, he settled down again at his post. There was nothing he could do anyhow. Not till he was relieved from this duty.

It was late, near time for the relief man, when two riders came from town. Slocum made himself ready for just about anything. It was dark, so they were nearly on him before he recognized Cash and Monkey.

"What the hell are you doing back here?" he asked.

"This is where we work," said Cash. "Where we live."

"You think that's still true after what you done?"

"You mean killing that fella?"

"You know that's what I mean."

"Hell, Slocum, it was a personal argument that led to a fight. He went for his gun. What could I do?"

"That ain't the way I heard it."

"Anyone who says Shotgun didn't go for his gun first is a damn liar," said Monkey.

"That's not what I meant," said Slocum. "He provoked it." Slocum pointed an accusing finger at Cash as he spoke those words. "He started that fight deliberately."

"All I need to say is that he drew first. You wanta make something out of it, Slocum?"

"I ain't the boss here," said Slocum. "We'll see what Townsend has to say."

Cash smirked and rode on. Monkey followed him. Soon Slocum's relief showed up, and Slocum mounted his horse and rode toward the ranch house. Under the circumstances, he was not surprised to find Townsend awake. There was no sign of Cash and Monkey. Slocum went up to the house and knocked on the door. Julie let him in.

"Have you seen Cash?" Slocum asked Townsend.

"I saw him," said the old man.

"Well?"

"Well, what? The sheriff wrote it down as self-defense. What else can I do but accept it?"

"You mean you let him stay on?"

"I got no other choice, Slocum. Damn it. Besides, we don't know what the hell Amos is up to. He might be bringing in more gunfighters for all we know. I might need Cash and his little buddy. Let it go."

"I guess if you don't give a damn, there's no reason I should. Hell," said Slocum. He turned and stomped out of the house. He was about to go down off the porch when Julie stepped out and stopped him.

"Wait," she said.

Slocum stood with his back to her. "What?"

"Don't be too hard on Uncle. He's had a rough time here lately. You and Cash helped him through it. He feels obligated. And he's afraid."

"I can understand that, but—"

"No buts. Just understand it. That's all."

"Yeah."

Julie walked around Slocum so she could face him. She reached up and pulled his face down to hers for a lingering kiss.

"You know," he said, "you could talk a man into most anything."

"That's not why I kissed you."

"I reckon I'm glad of that."

She kissed him again.

"I'm still looking forward to the right time," she said.

"Me too."

"John, sit down." They each took a chair. "I just don't want you going off in a foul mood. Sit here and talk with me for a while."

"You came out to talk with me," he said. "I guess I owe you that much."

"Don't stay because you owe me."

He took a deep breath and expelled it. "I won't," he said. "I'll stay on account of I enjoy your company. After what's happened this evening, I need some relaxation."

"Good. John?"

"What?"

"There's only one thing I'd like to add to what Uncle told you."

"What's that?"

"Watch Cash like a hawk. He's a cold-blooded son of a bitch."

11

The atmosphere at the Townsend ranch was thick with tension. Soon, everyone knew that Cash had killed Shotgun Stone. No one gave Cash hard looks. They were afraid that he would kill them too. They avoided him. For his part, Cash kept close to Monkey. He was the only one who would talk to Cash. Cash had seated himself beside Slocum the morning after the killing. Slocum was there ahead of him, eating his breakfast.

"Where we going today?" Cash had asked. "North pasture?"

"Yeah."

Slocum did not look at Cash. He had just continued eating his breakfast. Monkey came and sat on Cash's other side. "Morning, Cash," he said.

"How you doing this morning, kid?"

"I'm doing fine. How about you?"

"Fit as a fiddle, kid. Just great. Slocum says we're going back out to the north pasture today."

"All right."

"We ought to be done out there in another day or so. Wouldn't you say so, Slocum?"

"I reckon," said Slocum. He drained his coffee cup and

stood up to leave with no further words to either Cash or Monkey.

"What's the matter with him?" Monkey asked.

"Ah, he's got something up his ass." He looked around to make sure that no one was within earshot, and then he spoke to Monkey in hushed tones. "He ain't like us, kid. And if we don't do something about it real soon, he's going to be a problem."

"You mean—"

"I mean we got to kill ole Slocum. And right away." The kid took a sip of coffee and looked thoughtful. "Listen, kid," Cash went on, "I got to go to town this morning. You go on out to the north pasture with ole Slocum. Make up something to cover for me. Hell, tell him the truth. Tell him I had some business in town. Tell him I'll come around later in the day."

Monkey looked at Cash with a meaningful expression on his young face. "All right, Cash," he said.

Slocum rode past the ranch house on his way out, and he saw Julie on the porch. He rode over close to the porch and touched the brim of his hat. "Good morning," he said.

"Good morning. Do you have time for a cup of coffee?"

"I'd sure enough like to," said Slocum, "but I got to head on out to the north pasture. I got Cash and Monkey with me, and if I don't show, they'll just lay around talking about the notches on their guns."

"How about this evening?"

"I'll be looking forward to it." He turned his big Appaloosa to ride on, but she stopped him. "Slocum."

"Yes?"

"Remember what I told you."

"I'm always watchful, Julie," he said. "Don't worry about me."

Slocum did not see Monkey, so he headed on out alone. He had not ridden far, however, before he heard the pounding of hoofbeats behind him and turned to see Monkey coming. He did not bother to slow down. He let Monkey ride hard to catch up. When the young man pulled up beside him, neither of them spoke. Slocum had no more to say to Monkey. He had tried several times, but Cash had a tight hold on the kid. Slocum would speak to him if he had to tell him to do something, but not otherwise.

"You ain't asked me about Cash," Monkey said.

"No," said Slocum, "I ain't."

"He ain't with us this morning."

"I can see that."

"Don't you care how come he ain't with us?"

"Not particularly."

"Well, he had some business in town. He said he'd be along directly."

Slocum did not bother to answer. He would answer a direct question, but he would not make small talk. Not with Cash or Monkey. He was fed up with them. He wished they would move along. If he had been sure that the trouble with Amos was all over, he'd have moved on himself just to get away from them. He thought about Julie, though. He wasn't at all sure he wanted to move away from her just yet.

They made the rest of the ride out in silence. Monkey figured out that Slocum was in no mood to talk. Like Cash had said, he'd got something up his ass. Well, Monkey could play silent too. They reached the top of a rise overlooking the north pasture, and Slocum stopped riding and dismounted. He was looking around the range for any strays that might be out there. Monkey dismounted too and looked around, but he was not looking for cattle. He was looking to see if there was any sign of human beings who might see what was about to happen there. He saw none.

He dropped the reins of his horse and let them trail on the ground. Casually, he stepped away from the horse. He turned until he was directly facing Slocum. He had the early morning sun to his back. Everything was just right.

"Slocum," he said.

Slocum looked around, and he could see immediately what was on Monkey's mind.

"Don't be stupid," he said.

"I can take you."

"You can try."

"Go for your gun, Slocum."

"What difference does that make, kid?" Slocum said. "There are no witnesses out here."

Suddenly the kid made his move. He was fast. Slocum's Colt barked a split second before the kid's, and Slocum's bullet smashed the kid's right shoulder, causing him to drop his gun and fall to the ground. The kid's slug ripped flesh in Slocum's left arm.

"Damn," said the kid. "Damn, that was fast."

"I warned you," said Slocum.

"God damn you."

"Can you stand up?"

"I don't know," Monkey said. "I'll try. You gonna take me to a doctor?"

"I'll take you back to the ranch house. They can send for a doc if they want to. Get up."

Monkey turned as if to make an attempt to rise to his feet, but instead, he grabbed the revolver with his left hand and raised it to shoot. Slocum fired again. This time his bullet struck the kid in the forehead. Monkey dropped straight down on his face and lay there dead. Slocum ejected the spent shells from his Colt and reloaded. He picked up the kid and flung the body across the waiting horse. Then he retrieved the six-gun and poked it in his waistband. Taking the reins of the kid's horse, he remounted his Appaloosa and turned around to ride back to the ranch headquarters.

Cash was alone in a café in town, drinking coffee. He really had no business in town. He thought that if he gave a strong enough hint and left the kid alone with Slocum, the kid would take care of the problem. He wondered how long it would take for the kid to make his move. He wondered what might happen out there. He knew that Slocum was good, but he thought that the kid might be a little better. He wondered, though, if the kid would have the good sense not to give Slocum a fair shake.

He finished his coffee and walked outside to where his horse was tied. He stood for a moment, looking the town over. It was practically dead. A few people walked the sidewalks. A few horses were tied here and there. He mounted up and began the ride back to the Townsend ranch, going slow and taking his time.

"I believe Cash put him up to it," said Slocum. "He told me on the way out that Cash had business in town. Said he'd be along later. Then, when we got well out and away from everyone, he called me. He pushed it."

"I should have fired those two when Cash killed Shotgun," Townsend said.

"So what's going to happen now?" Julie asked. "What's left? For Cash to challenge you?"

"He won't do that," Slocum said. "He's more likely to try to shoot me from ambush."

"Slocum," Julie began, but he interrupted her.

"I know," he said. "Be careful."

"I don't like this," said Townsend. "We're thinning out our own ranks. And it's the top guns that's getting thinned."

"Yeah," said Slocum. "I'm wondering about something."

"What?"

"I'm wondering is it a plan. Is it just happening this way, or did Cash and the kid sell out?"

"You mean—"

"They went to work for Amos. That would explain Cash's killing Shotgun, and it would explain Monkey's attempt on me this morning."

"You mean they went to work for Amos," said Townsend, "but they kept on coming here as if—"

"As if everything was just the same," Slocum said. "What better way to get rid of folks?"

"All from the inside."

"Speaking of the devil," said Julie, "here comes Cash now."

Slocum turned around, ready for anything, as Cash rode up to the house. The newcomer quickly took in the situation. He saw the body on the horse, and he saw Slocum's stance. Townsend and Julie too were giving him hard looks. No one bothered to speak a greeting. Cash tried to play dumb.

"Is that Monkey there?"

"You know it is," said Slocum.

"What happened?"

"He tried to outgun me," said Slocum.

"We believe that you put him up to it," Townsend said. "You're no longer welcome here."

"You mean I'm fired?"

"You're fired."

"You going to take it just like that?" Slocum asked. "Or you gonna step down off that horse and fight me?"

"I don't want to fight you, Slocum. Hell, you saved my life."

"That was one big mistake I made. What's it gonna be?"

"I ain't gonna fight you," said Cash. He turned his horse and headed for the gate. Slocum pulled out his Colt and pointed it at Cash's back. He stood there until Cash was well out of six-gun range. Then he put it away again.

"Damn it," he said. "I couldn't do it. Not like that."

"I'm glad," said Julie. "I wouldn't have blamed you if you had shot him, but I'm glad you didn't."

"Ah, hell," said Slocum. "I should have. I'll likely live to regret it too. One of these days, I'm going to have to kill him."

Townsend called to one of the cowhands he spotted headed toward the corral, and told the man to take care of the body on the horse. The cowboy took horse and dead man away. Then Townsend said, "Slocum, come on up and sit with us a spell."

Slocum hesitated. Then he went up on the porch and took a seat.

"You reckon Cash will move on over to the White Hat now?" Townsend asked.

"There's no place else for him to go," said Slocum.

"Unless he pulls up stakes."

"He won't do that. I imagine that Amos has offered him a fair amount of money to finish us off."

"Other than Cash," Townsend said, "Amos has got only a few hands left."

"Yeah."

"You reckon we had oughta hit them first?"

"And hit them hard," said Slocum. "Let's do it right this time and finish the job."

"All right."

"When we hit them the first time," said Slocum, "we rode over early in the morning and attacked the ranch house and the bunkhouse. Right?"

"Right."

"We'll do the same thing again, but this time, we won't stop. We'll have some of the boys with torches, and we'll set fire to the houses. Burn them out. Kill them all."

"Every last son of a bitch," Townsend said. "When?"

"First thing in the morning."

Townsend called in all his hands and had them gathered around the big porch. He told them about Cash and Monkey and made sure that everyone knew what had happened. Then he told them Slocum's plan.

"You don't have to ride with us on this," he said. "You didn't hire on with me for this kind of work. But any of you

who want to go along will be more than welcome." Snaggletooth raised his hand. "No, Snaggletooth. I don't want
you to go. I want you to stay here with Julie."

Everyone else agreed to go along.

"All right, men," said Townsend. "Now, I'm turning this
whole business over to Slocum here, so from now till it's
done, listen to him."

Slocum stepped up on the porch. "We'll gather up right
here at five o'clock," he said. "Be mounted, and be well
armed. Check your weapons over real good tonight, and
make sure you have plenty of ammunition. We'll have
some torches here for some of you. Now go on and get
ready and try to get a good night's sleep. You'll need it."

The men dispersed to do as they had been told. Slocum
sat down heavily. Townsend offered him a cigar, and he
took it and lit it. "Thanks," he said.

"How about a little whiskey?"

"A little whiskey would be good," Slocum said.

Townsend turned to his niece. "Julie?"

"I'll get it," she said. She went into the house. Townsend
took a seat near Slocum.

"It'll all be over in the morning," Townsend said.

"Yeah."

Slocum puffed on the good cigar. Julie came back out
with a bottle and three glasses and poured whiskey all
around.

"That's good," said Slocum. "Thanks."

They sipped their whiskey for a while, and Townsend
excused himself to go to bed, leaving Slocum and Julie
alone on the porch.

12

Slocum was at the front porch ready to go before anyone else. He left his Appaloosa standing there and went up to take a chair on the porch and wait for the others. He sat there, not thinking about the coming fight but about his experience on that very porch the night before. After he had been left alone with Julie, he sat and visited with her. Then he had put an arm around her shoulders, and she had kissed him. It had been a long and lingering kiss, one that promised more to come. Slocum had not tried to follow up on that promise. He had not tried to go any further. There had been more kisses, but nothing else.

In the morning, the memories of the kisses and the promise stayed with him. They preyed on his mind and body. He wondered when he might expect that intriguing promise to be kept. He wondered if it would ever be kept. He was getting ready to go into a fight this morning, a fight to the finish, and he did not know how many men were on the other side. Neither did he know if they would be waiting for the attack or be caught by surprise. He did know that the White Hat outfit had one professional gunslinger in their ranks: Joe Cash, Slocum's former compadre. He was startled out of his reverie when the front door of the big house was opened and Townsend came out.

"You're out early, Slocum."

"Yeah."

"Ready to go?"

"I'm ready."

"Will they be waiting for us, do you think?"

"I think there's a good chance of it, with Cash on their side. He's a lot of things, but he's no fool."

"You're probably right about that. Slocum?"

Slocum looked over at the old man. He was grizzled and rugged, but he looked tired. There was a long pause.

"What is it?" Slocum asked.

"Slocum, I've prepared some papers. If anything should happen to me out there this morning, I want you to take over the ranch."

"Mr. Townsend—"

"Don't interrupt me, Slocum. Just listen. Like I said, if anything happens to me, I want you to take over. I got no son. All I have anymore is my niece, Julie. I drew up a paper giving you a half interest in the spread. That way, Julie won't be disinherited, but she'll have someone around to make sure that things go all right. I don't want no arguments. I'm just telling you. That's all. Here. Put this in your pocket."

Townsend handed Slocum a folded sheet of paper, which Slocum took. He held it a minute, looking at it without unfolding it. At last, he tucked it inside his shirt. "All right," he said. Nothing more. Some of the hands came riding up, and Julie stepped out on the porch. Slocum stood up and took the hat off his head.

"Good morning," he said.

"Good morning."

The old man did not miss the looks that his niece and Slocum exchanged. That was fine with him. Maybe, he thought, if something should happen to him, his paper would keep Slocum around long enough for nature to take its course. That would be just fine. Other cowhands rode up. Townsend stood up and walked to the edge of the porch.

"Someone bringing me a horse?" he asked.

"Billy Boy's saddling your favorite, boss," answered a cowhand.

"Soon as he brings it around, we'll ride," said Townsend.

"Everyone know what to do?" Slocum asked.

The answer from the waiting hands was affirmative. Julie put a hand on Slocum's shoulder, while her uncle watched out of the corner of his eye. "Be careful," she said.

"I always am," Slocum answered.

Billy Boy came riding from the corral, leading an extra horse.

"Uncle," said Julie. Townsend looked directly at her then. "You don't have to go with them, do you?" she asked him.

"Yes," he said. "I do."

She sighed, a long and weary sigh, and said, "All right then. You be careful too. I want you to come back." Then she looked out over the crowd. "I want all of you to come back. All of you, watch yourselves. Be careful." Then she turned and walked back inside the house. Townsend and Slocum walked down from the porch and mounted their horses. They took the lead, as the others all turned their mounts. Townsend looked at Slocum.

"You're in charge," he said.

"Let's ride," shouted Slocum, and the whole bunch took off at once, headed for the main gate.

They did not ride fast. There was no need to wear out the horses. It was still early. The sun was not quite up in the sky. The far eastern horizon was just beginning to show some color. They rode at a leisurely but deliberate pace. The faces of the riders were all hard and determined. Each man knew what he was riding into. Each man knew that it could be his last day on earth. But each man was also determined that this would be the last day of the range war between the Townsend spread and the White Hat Ranch. When they came to the gate that would lead them onto the White Hat property, Slocum spotted a lookout.

He jerked out his Colt and fired a shot that dropped the man instantly. The riders did not slow down. They kept on track toward the main house. About halfway down the lane, Slocum picked up the pace. As they drew close to the ranch house, a couple of cowhands came running out of the bunkhouse at the back. They were armed, and they ran toward the main house. Slocum dropped one with a shot, and Townsend dropped the other. Windows of the main house were thrown open. Guns were poked out of the windows and shots were fired.

"Dismount and take cover," Slocum shouted.

It looked disorganized, as each man abandoned his mount and raced for the nearest protection. Bullets smacked into the ground around them as they ran. One Townsend horse was killed in the first volley, but no men were hurt. There were plenty of shots being fired, but they were all wasted. Crouched behind a tree, Slocum looked around for any sign of Cash. He saw none.

The fight was going nowhere. Nothing was being accomplished except the fruitless expending of ammunition. He had to think of something else, some other way of bringing this whole thing to a head, and fast. Ducking low, he ran back farther into the trees in front of the big house. He ducked behind another tree and waited till he was sure that no one had a bead on him. Then he turned to his left and ran some more. He came to the edge of the trees and found himself perhaps twenty yards from the bunkhouse. He knew that there were still some hands in there. He wasn't sure how many. In a crouch, he ran for it.

Shots kicked up dirt around him as he sped across the

empty space, but he reached the wall of the bunkhouse un-hurt. Crashing against it to stop himself, he stood, holding his Colt ready and looking around. He could hear voices from inside.

"It's Slocum," someone said. "He's right outside."

"Well, go out and get the son of a bitch."

The second was the voice of Joe Cash. Slocum's heart thrilled at the sound.

"You go get him," said the first voice. "You're the god-damned gunfighter, ain't you? He was your pardner, wasn't he?"

"I'll go down to the far window there," said Cash. "I'll make some noise to get his attention. You go out the front door and shoot him in the back. Nothing to it. Go on now."

Then all was silent. Slocum had to act quickly. He wasn't sure if those were the only two in the bunkhouse. Crouching down, he took a match out of his pocket and lit some dry grass along the base of the wall. He watched it for a few seconds as the flames took hold. Then he heard a window break to his left, and he knew that it was Cash try-ing to create a diversion for the other hand. He looked to his right, and in another instant, he saw the man come around the corner of the building, a rifle raised and ready to shoot. Slocum snapped off a round from his Colt. The man jerked and fell back. Slocum could see nothing but one boot showing from around the corner. He turned and ran toward the broken window.

The flames had begun to lap at the wall and smoke was beginning to billow. Slocum could hear the sound of men running out the front door, shooting as they ran. He thought that he could distinguish the sound of bullets being returned by Townsend's men. He had bigger prey on his mind. Reach-ing the broken window, he boldly stood up straight and looked inside. There was no one in sight. He could see a back door standing open. Quickly, he ran around to the back of the building. There was no sign of life. He stepped inside.

One man who had been hidden from his view took a shot at him. It came close. He heard it whiz past his left ear. He fired back quickly, and his shot took the man in the chest, dropping him instantly. He stood ready, looking around. There was no one else. The flames were consuming the wall of the bunkhouse by then, and beginning to eat at the roof. Soon the building would be a heap of ashes. He went back outside and looked around. He could see no sign of life back there. He ran around the building to discover several bodies on the ground: the men who had run from the burning building had been picked off neatly by Townsend's crew. Fighting was still raging around the main house. Slocum ran back over there, bullets dancing around him as he ran. Slocum hit the dirt behind some stacked bales of hay, winding up right beside old Townsend.

"You all right?" Townsend asked.

"Yeah. How about you?"

"I'm just fine," the old man said. "You fire that bunkhouse?"

"I did."

"Damn good work."

"Any sign of Cash?" Slocum asked.

"I ain't seen him," said Townsend.

"Any of our boys hit?"

"Two wounded. Not bad. What do we do now?"

Slocum thought for a moment. "How about the same thing I did over there?"

"Fire?"

"Yeah. Only this time, I won't leave a back door open. Have the men give me a hell of a cover."

"Boys," Townsend shouted. "Hit them hard with all you got."

Everyone started firing at once, and Slocum ran again. He ran back to the bunkhouse, where he picked up two burning boards. Then he ran for the backside of the main house. He broke a window with one board and tossed it inside.

Then he moved to the back door and carefully placed the second board at the bottom of the door. Then he backed off, Colt in hand, watching the door. The flames caught on nicely. Soon the door and the wall around it were blazing. He could also see through the window, fire building up inside. He did not think anyone would try to get out that way, but he couldn't be sure. He decided to stay for a bit and be ready.

He heard more shots from the front of the building, but he could not know whether or not they meant that the men in the house were trying to escape. He waited until he was sure the flames in back were large enough to prevent escape that way. Then he ran around the house again. He saw some bodies on the ground out there: men who had tried to get out. As he stood watching, another man came running out the front door, screaming and firing as he ran. He staggered and fell from several shots.

Slocum ducked low and ran again, back to the bales of hay that covered Townsend. He threw himself down again beside the old man. He was panting for breath. Townsend ducked low behind the bales and looked at Slocum.

"Not hurt?"

"No."

"You got them, all right," Townsend said. "Most of them's come out already. Most of them's dead."

"What about Bob Amos?"

"Ain't seen him yet."

"What about Cash?"

"Nope."

Having caught his breath again, Slocum turned and peered up over the bales. He could tell that there were at least two men left in the burning house. They continued to fire out the windows. Townsend's men returned fire.

"They won't be in there for long now," Slocum said.

"They got to come out or burn," said Townsend.

"Yeah."

Suddenly a man came running through the already opened front door. He was holding a six-gun in each hand, and he fired both as he appeared. He was firing in any direction. He did not have a target. He was frantic, desperate. He did not have a chance, but the men who were opposed to him had no mercy. He staggered and then crumpled in a heap, at least six bullets in him.

"Townsend. Slocum."

The shouting came from inside the burning house. Slocum answered it.

"What do you want?"

"Don't shoot. I'm coming out."

"That you, Amos?" yelled Townsend.

"It's me. Don't shoot."

"Who else is in there with you?" Slocum called out.

"No one. Just me."

"Come out with your hands up high," said Slocum. "Nobody shoots."

It was silent except for the roaring and crackling of the flames. All eyes were on the front door as Bob Amos, his hands held high, stepped out. He walked slowly forward to escape the heat from inside his burning ranch house. Slocum and Townsend, holding their guns ready, stood up.

"Keep him covered," said Slocum, and he walked over to meet Amos. He looked him over quickly and determined that he was not armed. Then he glanced at the house. It was nearly consumed. No one alive was in there. He called over his shoulder to the others.

"Come on out," he said. "It's all over here."

As Townsend and the rest of the crew came out of hiding, Slocum looked Amos in the face. "Where's Cash?"

"I don't know," said Amos. "He was out in the bunkhouse. I ain't seen him since you showed up. Likely you burned him."

Slocum knew better than that, but he didn't say anything about it. As far as Townsend was concerned, the war was over. They would deliver Amos to the sheriff in town and let the law handle it from here. But Slocum's war was not over, and it would not be until he had found Cash. He could take it that Cash had switched sides. There were lots of gunmen who would do that for a reason. It didn't bother him that Cash would have taken a shot at him for money after having pretended to be his friend. He had saved Cash's life, and Cash had turned on him. He could let all that go. What he could not forgive was Cash's turning the young cowhand, Monkey, into a gunslinger and siccing him on Slocum. He could not forgive Cash for having made him kill the kid. He knew that he would have to go after Cash.

Two of the cowhands had tied Amos's hands behind his back, and Slocum said, "Get him on his horse. We'll take him to town."

"Why bother?" someone said. "Let's just hang him."

13

Slocum considered protesting, but then he reconsidered. He figured there was really nothing he could do about it. Old Townsend was obviously all for it, and besides, what difference would it make in the end? Amos might have been killed in the fight. If he were to be arrested and tried, he might be hanged anyway, and if by some chance he should get off free after the trial, likely someone from Townsend's bunch would be waiting to kill him. Maybe even Slocum. He stood back and let it happen.

Amos's hands were tied behind his back, and he was forced into a saddle. In the meantime, a cowhand tossed a rope over a tree branch. The horse bearing the doomed man was led to the tree, and the noose placed around the neck of Amos.

"You can't do this," Amos protested. "Stop it. Take me to jail."

No one paid any attention to him. In the minds of the Townsend hands, the war would be over with this one simple act. Someone slapped the horse on the rear, and it bolted. Amos was jerked back out of the saddle in mid-sentence. He gagged. His tongue stuck out. His face turned blue as he kicked and squirmed and twisted. His cock got hard and bulged in his jeans, and his bowels relaxed. He shit his pants. With one last kick of both legs, he expired. Slocum mounted his Appaloosa and turned to ride away. The rest were still standing around the corpse. Slocum did not look back.

He rode straight to town and stopped in front of the saloon. He tied his horse there at the hitch rail and went inside. At the bar, he ordered a bottle of bourbon and a glass. He paid for it and took it to a table. He turned the first glass down, drinking it almost all at once. Then he poured a second glass. There was a bad taste in his mouth that he had to get rid of. He had no good feelings for Bob Amos. He might easily have killed the son of a bitch himself, but the way in which Amos had met his end disgusted him.

He finished his second glass of whiskey and poured a third. Honey Pot came down the stairs and saw him. She smiled and moved to his table.

"Like some company?" she said.

Slocum looked up at her. He thought about sending her away, but he did not have the energy. "Suit yourself," he said.

"I ain't seen you in here for a while," she said. "How come you be here drinking all by yourself?"

"It's a long story, Honey Pot," Slocum said. "I don't think you'd be interested."

"You might be surprised," she said.

"Yeah? Well, I ain't interested in talking about it."

"Where are your two buddies?"

"Buddies?"

"You know, Monkey and Cash."

"One's dead," he said. "The other one's run off."

"What?"

"I think you heard me right."

"Well, what happened?"

"I told you I don't want to talk about it."

"Okay," she said.

"Have a drink, Honey Pot. If you want to talk, let's talk about something else."

Honey Pot waved a hand at the barkeep, who brought her a glass. Slocum poured it full of whiskey. Honey Pot picked it up and sipped from it.

"Say," she said, "why don't we take this bottle and go upstairs?" She waited, but got no response. "You're in some kind of a low mood, ain't you? We don't have to do nothing but sit and drink. We can talk if you want. It's more private than down here."

Slocum thought for a moment. He looked around the room. It occurred to him that Townsend or some of his crew might come in to celebrate. Taking the bottle in one hand and his glass in the other, he stood up. "Let's go," he said. Honey Pot took her glass and stood up to walk with him. They went up the stairs and into a room. Honey Pot shut the door behind them. Slocum took a chair, placing the bottle on the small table there. There was one other chair in the room, and Honey Pot pulled it over to the table. She sat across from Slocum. Slocum finished his drink and poured himself another. Honey Pot still had some in her glass.

"Slocum?" said Honey Pot.

He looked up at her over his glass.

"I wish you'd say something."

"I'm going to be moving on," he said.

"How come?"

"The war's over. They hanged Bob Amos this morning."

"Hanged him? You mean—"

"Lynched."

"Oh, God. And Monkey and Cash?"

"Monkey's dead. I killed him."

"Jesus," she said. "How come?"

He didn't know what it was that had finally loosened his tongue, maybe the whiskey, maybe Honey Pot's sympathetic attitude. Likely her good looks had something to do with it. Whatever it was, he kept talking. "Cash took Monkey and went over to the other side. More money. Excitement. Hell, I don't know, but they went. Then Monkey forced me into a showdown. I killed him."

"God. That's awful."

"We raided the White Hat this morning. Wiped them out. All except Amos and Cash. The crew strung Amos up right off. We never did see Cash. He's run off."

"Then it really is over?"

"It's over for Townsend," Slocum said. "It ain't over for me."

"Cash?"

"I'm going after him," Slocum said. "It's his fault I killed that kid. He won't get away with it."

"When will you go?"

"I don't know," he said. "I'd have left already, except for the hanging. I wasn't in the mood. I guess I'll get drunk and then sleep it off. Then I'll go looking for him."

Honey Pot stood up and dragged her chair around the table. Then she sat down again right next to Slocum. She put an arm around his shoulders and pulled his head down on her breast. He didn't fight it. It felt good there on that soft but firm titty as it rose and fell with her breathing.

"You're a good man, John Slocum," she said. "Too good for these parts, these times."

"I don't know about that," he said.

"Damn sight too good for the likes of me."

Slocum thought about Julie Townsend. She would be thrilled at the news about Bob Amos. He lifted his head up and leaned in to kiss Honey Pot. He kissed her tenderly, like a lover, not like a customer. Then he pulled her head down onto his chest and held her close.

"Don't ever say that," he told her. "You're as good as anyone. Better than some I can think of."

He had not wanted this, but in spite of himself, he felt a stirring in his loins. Just then, she turned her head, and he kissed her again. This time, the kiss was long, lingering, passionate. Their lips parted, and their tongues dueled. Slocum embraced her tightly, and her own fingers dug into his back. At last they broke apart, and Honey Pot stood up. She started to loosen her bodice. Slocum sat still, watching her as she slipped out of her dress. He reached out both hands and pressed them against her lovely heaving tits. Her mouth opened, and she breathed deeply.

He stood up then and started to undress himself. They finished at about the same time, and then they moved together. They stood, naked, embracing, kissing, their hands roaming around over each other's bodies. At last, Honey Pot broke away. She crawled onto the bed, and as she did, Slocum admired her round ass cheeks and the tuft of hair that he could see just below them. In the middle of the mattress, she turned and lay down on her back, allowing her legs to flop apart casually, reaching her arms up to invite him in. Slocum's rod stood up.

He moved in on her, allowed his weight to press down on her body, feeling the intense pleasure of her touch all the way up and down. As he kissed her again, she reached with both hands for his cock and balls. She held them and fondled them, marveling at the length and stiffness of the thing, and then she guided it deftly into her waiting, wet hole.

"Ah," Slocum moaned as he slid into her depths. He drove in all the way, and Honey Pot bucked up underneath, making sure that she had it all, that it was rammed in fully. They pressed hard against one another for a long moment. Then Slocum began to withdraw. He was about ready to slip out before he shoved it in again, slowly, savoring the intense feeling all along the way. He did that again and again, and gradually built up speed. Soon he was ramming himself in and out of her, and she was bucking and humping underneath.

"Oh, God, oh, God," she said. "Fuck me, Slocum. Fuck me good."

He humped harder and faster, his own torso slapping against hers with each thrust as she rose to meet him. He pressed his lips against hers. Their mouths opened as they seemed to try to devour one another. Suddenly, Slocum pulled out. She was startled for an instant, until he reached for her waist and turned her over. Immediately, she pulled her knees up under her, thrusting her ass toward him. He probed from behind for her slippery cunt, and she once again reached back between her legs to grip the hard cock and guide it home.

Slocum began driving hard again, and she responded. He could see her lovely tits jiggle underneath her as their bodies smacked together, and it was lovely to watch her ass cheeks jounce as he smashed into them over and over again. Then, all at once, he felt the intense pressure build up in his balls. He humped faster, desperate now for release. Then it came. He spurted into her, again and again. With each thrust, he shot another load deep into her channel.

"Oh, God, I feel it," she said. "I can feel your come."

At last he was done. On his knees behind her, he stopped still, panting. He was spent. His cock slowly lost its hardness. It shriveled inside her until it slipped out. Slocum fell over sideways, landing on his back beside her. She leaned over to kiss him, and slowly lay down, her breasts on his chest, the rest of her lying beside him.

"That was just too good," she said.

"You can say that again for me," said Slocum.

Then they lay side by side, quiet, catching their breath, for some time, neither one needing to say anything, neither one worrying about the time. At last, Honey Pot rose up slowly. She moved to the table where a bowl of water waited, and she dipped a towel into the water, then wrung it

out. Moving back to the bed, she sat down and began washing him off. She lingered over the job for a long time, and
Slocum let her. It felt good. At last, the pleasant job finished,
she stood up and swiped between her own legs. Then
she tossed the towel back onto the table.

"You want a drink?" she asked.

"Yeah," he said. "Thanks."

She poured two drinks and brought them over to the
bed. As she sat down on the edge of the bed, Slocum pulled
himself up to a sitting position. He sipped the whiskey
this time. It was good. Thoughts of Julie Townsend, the
Townsend ranch crew, the ugly lynching of Bob Amos,
even the betrayal of Joe Cash had all left his mind, at least
for a time.

"You're a wonder-worker, Honey Pot," he said.

"You feeling better?"

"I can't recall a time I ever felt this good."

"That's what I like to hear," she said. "Slocum?"

"Yeah?"

"My name's Jolene."

"What?"

"Jolene. That's my real name. I just want you to know."

"Jolene," he said. "I like that. It's a nice name."

"Thanks," she said. She leaned over and kissed him tenderly on the lips. As she moved back, he lifted his glass
and finished it. Jolene took the empty glass away from him.
"Another?" she asked.

"Not another drink," he said.

She looked him in the face and smiled, took one more
sip of her own glass, put both glasses on the table, and
turned back to him. She leaned over him again, kissing
him. She put her hands on his chest as she stretched out
over his body. Down below, she could feel him responding
favorably to the situation. She let it rise on its own, continuing to kiss him for a long time. At last, she broke away
from the kiss and moved down a bit to kiss his chest, to lick

his nipples. She slid a bit more and licked his belly as she went. At last she was down as far as she wanted to go.

She gripped the hard cock with her right hand and with her left, balanced the heavy balls in her palm. The head of the cock was right before her eyes. It bucked in her grip. She squeezed it harder, and it bucked again. She leaned in closer, sticking out her tongue, and she licked it. It bucked furiously as Slocum thrust upward. She smiled, and she licked again.

Slocum knew what was coming, and he wanted it badly, but she continued to tease, now licking all along its length. She turned her head sideways and bit it between her lips from the side, then slid up and down. Slocum began to hump and thrust as if he were inside her again, and at last, she moved her head again, she opened her lips wide, and she took the head in her mouth. It was sudden and unexpected and incredibly wonderful, and Slocum gasped at the sensation. He thrust again, and she lowered her head as he did, taking the entire length into her mouth, down her throat. Then she began in earnest. She moved her head up and down to the rhythm of his thrusts, until at last he exploded again, and she swallowed each large spurt until he was done. Then she moved off. She looked at the cock she gripped in her hand. She squeezed it and milked it, bringing out a last drop, and she licked it clean.

Slocum was sober, and his head was clear. He rode back out to the Townsend ranch for his gear. He managed to avoid anyone until he was all packed and ready to ride out. As he moved past the ranch house, Townsend came out onto the porch.

"Slocum," Townsend called out.

Slocum hesitated, then rode over to the porch. He nodded at the old man.

"You ain't leaving, are you?"

"My job's done here," said Slocum.

"Well, yeah, the war's over. We won it. But you hired on as a cowhand. I didn't hire you just on account of the war. You're welcome to stay as long as you like."

"Sorry, Townsend. I got things to do elsewhere."

Julie came out on the porch just then. She saw what was going on, and she just looked at Slocum with curiosity.

"Going after Cash, ain't you?" asked Townsend.

"You guessed it right."

"Well, hold on a minute. You got some pay coming."

Slocum thought about telling the old man to shove his pay up his ass, as the image of the demise of Bob Amos came back into his mind. He thought about it, but he kept his mouth shut. It probably wouldn't be the bloodiest money he had ever accepted, and he would need it along the trail. He sat still in the saddle, waiting for the old man to bring out his pay.

14

While Townsend was still inside the house, Julie stepped over to the edge of the porch. She stood silent for a while just looking at Slocum sitting there on his horse. At last, she spoke, and her voice was icy cold. "So you're leaving us," she said.

"That's the idea."

"What for?"

"Like I said, the job's done."

"I thought we had some unfinished business, you and me. Did you forget about that?"

"I remember all right, but I reckon I was wrong about it."

"What changed your mind?" she asked. "The lynching?"

"I'd say that had something to do with it."

"I thought you were a tougher man than that. We were at war here. You'd have shot him down, wouldn't you?"

"Under the right circumstances."

"Why should you give a damn about what happened to Bob Amos?"

"I don't particularly," Slocum said. "I just don't hold with the way it was done."

"And you won't change your mind?"

"No. I won't."

Townsend came back out, and Julie turned on her heel and went into the house. She's as cold and hard as her uncle, Slocum thought. He rode up as close to the porch as he could get. Townsend held out the cash and Slocum reached for it. He tucked the money into his shirt pocket. "Thanks," he said dryly. He turned the Appaloosa and rode slowly away from the house. His thoughts were mixed as he rode. He had taken on a job, and he had done it. The side for which he had fought had won the war. He should feel good about that. But along the way, he had been betrayed by Cash. He'd been forced to kill a snot-nosed kid, and finally, he had witnessed a lynching. He did not feel good about the victory.

As he reached the big front gate, he paused. He really had no idea where he was going. He was on the trail of Joe Cash, but he did not know where the son of a bitch had gone. He thought for a moment.

Cash was not the type to ride a long trail unless he had to. Likely, he would head for the nearest town. He had no chances of employment nearby, and besides that, he surely no longer felt safe in these parts. The closest town that Slocum knew about was three days' ride to the west. It was worth a try. He turned the big Appaloosa's head toward the setting sun.

Slocum rode the rest of the day away with no indication that he was on the right trail, no sign that he was not. He did not pass any riders along the way. Toward nightfall, he stopped to camp for the night. He fixed himself a small meal and some coffee and turned in early. In the morning, he started his day with only coffee. He would wait for a meal until around noon when he would be really hungry. About mid-morning he saw a rider coming at him from the west. As the two approached each other, Slocum hailed the other.

"Howdy."

"Howdy, stranger," the man replied. "Traveling far?"

"To the next town, whatever it is."

"It's called Kiowa Gap," the man said. "About two days' ride west."

"You come from there?"

"Yep."

"You didn't see a man called Cash, by any chance?" Slocum asked.

"Don't recall the name."

"He's a man about my age, maybe a little younger. About my size too. Usually wears black and wears his hair long and his guns low."

"Yeah. There was a feller like that in town. You hunting him, are you?"

"I'd like to cross his trail again," said Slocum.

"Well, he was there."

"Do you mean he's gone?"

"Nope. I mean, he was there whenever I was there. Don't know if he's still there or not."

"I see."

"A friend of yours?"

"I know him," said Slocum.

The man studied Slocum's face for a moment; then he said, "Good luck to you."

"Thanks," said Slocum. The two men rode on their own respective ways. So Cash was up ahead about two more days in the town called Kiowa Gap. Slocum decided that he could hurry up his pace a little, maybe cut the ride down to a day and a half and hope that Cash would still be hanging around. He moved on. The road got a little busier as he drew closer to Kiowa Gap. He passed three more riders that day, and one wagon with a man and a boy in it. He talked to each of the travelers. The two in the wagon had not seen Cash, but the three men on horseback all remembered him, one by name.

"I got in a card game with him," the man said. "He damn near cleaned me out. I think the son of a bitch was cheating me, but I couldn't catch him at it. Couldn't prove it. Say, is he a friend of yours?"

"Let's just say I know him," Slocum said.

The man looked at Slocum's cold eyes, and he thought that maybe he knew what was up. "I hope he's still there when you get to town," he said. "I hope you catch up with him."

"Thanks," said Slocum. He camped on the trail again that night and got up for an early start in the morning. That day the traffic was heavy. He passed at least a dozen travelers. After questioning the first four, he let it go. Cash was definitely in Kiowa Gap, unless he had just left, and if he had done that, he could not be far ahead. Slocum hurried on. He was itching to face the man, anxious for a showdown. Cash deserved a quick trip to the next world, whatever and wherever it might be, and Slocum wanted to be the one to send him on his way.

He reached Kiowa Gap about noon. It was a small one-saloon town. It had a hotel that wasn't much either. If Cash was still in town, he wouldn't be hard to find. Slocum located the livery stable without any problems and put up his horse. He paid the man there in advance. Then he walked to the saloon. He stepped cautiously inside, looking the room over. There was a card game in progress, but Cash was not in it. He was nowhere in sight.

Slocum walked over to the bar and ordered himself a shot of whiskey. When the bartender poured it, Slocum asked him, "You know a man named Cash?"

The bartender looked at Slocum for a moment. "Yeah," he said. "I know who he is."

"He around?"

"He was."

"You mean he's pulled out?"

"Early this morning," said the barkeep. "He had several of the local men pissed off at him. They thought he was cheating at cards. Couldn't quite catch him, though. I guess he got the idea and decided it wasn't too safe for him around here."

"Just this morning, you say?"

"That's right."

Slocum downed his drink. "Hit me again," he said. "He can't be but a few hours ahead of me then."

"I'd say three, four hours ahead."

"Do you know which way he rode out?"

"There's only two ways out of Kiowa Gap," said the man. "East and west. Which way'd you come from?"

"I rode in from the east," Slocum said.

"And you didn't see him?"

"No."

"Then he rode out west."

Slocum emptied his glass and put some change on the bar. "Much obliged," he said, and he turned to leave. He stopped and turned back, though, when the bartender spoke again.

"There's just one little problem," said the barkeep.

Slocum looked at the man. "What's that?" he asked.

"About five miles out of town on the road going west, you got a choice. There's a crossroad. Turn north and you ride into Trail's End in about twenty miles. Turn south and you're headed for Sunflower. About the same distance. Maybe a little farther."

"I see."

"If I was you," the man said, "if it was me hunting that Cash feller, I'd head south."

"Sunflower?"

"Yeah. It's a little wilder town than Trail's End. A little bigger. More opportunities for an hombre like that Cash, if you get my drift."

"I get you," said Slocum. "Where can I get a meal here?"

"Right across the street. Only place in town."

Slocum crossed the street and had a meal that he had not cooked for himself. That was about all he could say for it.

The steak was tough, and the bread was hard and dry. The coffee tasted like it had been in the pot for three days. He ate the meal, though, and drank the coffee. He paid for the wretched meal and left. At least he wasn't hungry. The Appaloosa had not spent much time in the stable, but he had been well fed, likely better than Slocum had been, and rested up some. Slocum saddled up and hit the trail again. He figured that Cash had long since hit the crossroad and turned either north or south. He had nothing more to go on than the bartender's assumption that Cash would have headed south to Sunflower. He decided that he would do the same. If it should turn out that Cash had not gone to Sunflower, he would turn around and head the other way. It wouldn't be much of a loss. A few hours at the most. Slocum was getting anxious, though, to bring this business to a close.

He reached Sunflower in the early evening. Watching carefully as he rode into town, he did not recognize any horse. Cash could have changed his horse, though, at most any time, maybe as early as when he ran away from White Hat on that bloody morning. Slocum again looked up a stable first thing, and saw to it that his horse was well taken care of. Then he walked down the main street of the town. He could see two, no, three saloons. Chances were that Cash was in one of them. He headed for the nearest one, The Snappy Garter.

He had already decided that Cash or no, he would spend the night there in Sunflower, but first he would look the place over for any sign of Cash. He ordered a glass of good bourbon whiskey, paid the barkeep, and then he said, "I'm looking for a man who calls himself Cash."

The bartender stared at Slocum.

"Well, have you seen him?"

"Not that I recall."

Slocum took his glass to a table and sat down. The

Snappy Garter was doing good business. About half of the tables were occupied, and the bar was lined with cowhands and other types. Saloon girls flitted from one man to another until they found one who would buy their drinks or go with them to one of the rooms in the back. Slocum studied the crowd, but he saw no sign of Cash. Well, there were two more saloons. He finished his drink and walked out of the place. He did not see the bartender speak low in the ear of a cowhand standing at the bar behind him. The cowhand downed his drink and turned to hurry out of the saloon just after Slocum.

Slocum stopped for a moment on the sidewalk outside to study the street. There was a hotel just across the street from where he stood. It would keep. The other two saloons, Whiskey River and Rogers's Saloon, were about the same distance away from him, but Whiskey River was on the other side of the street. He considered for a moment, and then he decided to cross over to Whiskey River. That sounded like the proper place for the likes of Cash. Anyhow, he would give it a try. The cowhand from The Snappy Garter had already crossed the street and gone into Whiskey River, but Slocum had paid no attention to the man. There were cowhands going in and out of all three saloons, and he did not know any of them. He stepped into the street.

He had to pause as a man on horseback rode by, and halfway across the street, he waited for a wagon to pass. He heard a commotion behind him and looked over his shoulder to see a fight begin just outside Rogers's Saloon. He strained his eyes to see if Cash was involved or was watching, but he saw no sign of the man. Slocum figured if Cash had been inside Rogers's Saloon, he would have stepped out to watch the fight. With Cash not part of it, it was none of his business. He turned his back to go on inside Whiskey River. He pushed open the batwing doors, stepped in, and started to look around, and he was startled by the first thing he saw. He was met with the image of Cash behind a gun that was already leveled at him, already cocked. He did not even have time to reach for his own Colt before the blast made his ears ring, before the impact struck his chest, before the light faded and his consciousness was gone.

15

He woke up in a strange bed, in a strange room. He felt barely alive. His eyes opened slowly and tried to take in the unknown surroundings. Gradually, things came back to him. He remembered stepping into the saloon. He recalled the image of Cash there before him, gun cocked, in hand, and already up and pointed at him. He remembered the blast and the thud, and then he knew nothing. He had no idea how he had been brought to this room or whose room it was. Who had doctored him? He did not know. He raised his head just a bit to look down at his chest, and he saw the bandages, but then he let his head drop back down on the pillow. The effort had been almost too much for him. He drifted back into unconsciousness with a head full of unanswered questions.

The next time he woke up, he was conscious of only a terrible hunger, a gnawing in his gut. He tried to sit up, but it was no use. He had not the strength. He lay there staring at the strange room around him. His chest hurt, but not unbearably. He wondered how long he had been there like that. He thought about trying once again to rise, but before he had committed himself fully to the notion, the door opened and a woman stepped into the room. She was matronly, but pleasant enough. As soon as she saw that he was awake, she smiled.

"How are you feeling?" she asked him.

"Where am I?"

"You're in Dr. Spencer's office," she said. "I'm his nurse, sort of. My name's Peggy Sue."

"How long have I—"

"You've been out for several days. Now answer my questions. First, how are you feeling?"

"I'm—weak," Slocum said. "And hungry. Awful hungry."

"I'll tell the doctor that you're awake and ask him if I can fix something for you to eat. Just lie still. I'll be back real soon."

Peggy Sue left the room, and in another couple of minutes, the doctor came in. He went straight to Slocum's bedside and pulled up a chair. "I told Peggy Sue to fix you up some nice broth and some coffee. We don't want you eating too much too fast. I was worried for the first few days about you ever waking up again. You were almost killed, you know."

"Yeah. It started coming back to me."

"Can you sit up?"

"I tried once. Didn't get very far."

"You want to try again?"

Slocum strained, but as he tried to sit up, the pain shot through his chest. Doc Spencer put an arm behind him to help, and soon he had Slocum sitting upright. He put pillows behind his back.

"How's that?" the doc asked.

Slocum sucked in a few deep breaths. "It's okay," he said.

"I think you're going to come out of this all right," said Spencer. "It'll take a while yet for you to really mend, but you're already way past the worst of it. Yeah, you'll be just fine, if we don't starve you to death first."

"That's what I feel like is happening," said Slocum.

Peggy Sue came in with a bowl and a cup on a tray, and

she put the tray on Slocum's lap. Doc stood up and moved out of the way.

"Do you need help?" Peggy Sue asked.

"No, thank you, ma'am," said Slocum. "I can manage."

Had the broth not been so hot, Slocum would have slurped it all down at once, but he had to eat it with the spoon. The bowl was soon empty, though, and he drank the coffee. Peggy Sue had stayed in the room to watch him.

"Want more?" she asked.

What Slocum really wanted was a beefsteak, but he said, "Yes, ma'am. I do."

Peggy Sue fetched more broth and more coffee, and Slocum took it all in. This time she did not offer more, even though he was still hungry. Doc had said not too much or too fast. Something like that. It was a little later when Peggy Sue came back into the room.

"The sheriff's here," she said. "Do you feel up to talking with him?"

"Sure," said Slocum.

Peggy Sue ducked out of the room. In another moment, a tall, middle-aged man with a potbelly stepped into the room. He sported a handlebar mustache, and he was wearing two pieces of a three-piece suit. A star was pinned on the vest. A six-gun was holstered at his right side.

"I'm Ham Vance," he said. "Sheriff. Doc says you're doing better. Says it won't hurt if we talk a little. That all right with you?"

"Yeah," Slocum said. "It's all right."

"What's your name?"

"John Slocum."

Vance sat down in the chair that Doc had vacated earlier. "Seems like I might have heard that name before somewhere," he said.

"You might have," said Slocum.

"You're a gunfighter."

"I've been in some fights."

"That probably explains what happened to you."

"I reckon it might."

"Tell me about it," said Vance.

"There ain't much to tell," said Slocum. "I stepped in the door, and Cash shot me. I didn't even know he was in there."

"Cash? That his name?"

"It's the only one I know for him. Joe. Joe Cash."

"Joe Cash. Is he wanted?"

"I couldn't answer that."

"Are you wanted?"

"Not that I know of."

"How come this Joe Cash shoot you like that?" asked Vance. "I'd say he was trying to kill you. How come?"

"I don't know, unless he's figured out that I mean to kill him."

"What for?"

"I just think he needs killing. That's all."

"You ain't being much help to me here, Slocum."

"What kind of help do you want, Sheriff? You got Cash in jail?"

"No. We chased him, but he got out of town."

"Are you going after him?"

"He's out of my jurisdiction."

"I don't know what I could be doing to help you then. I'm John Slocum. He's Joe Cash. He shot me and ran off. If I can ever get up out of this bed again, I'm riding after him. That's about it."

Vance stood up. "Well, Slocum," he said, "I hope you do get up out of that bed real soon, 'cause when you do, I want you to ride out of my town. Gunfighters are always trouble."

"I reckon so, Sheriff," Slocum said as Vance was walking out of the room.

So Cash had run out of town as soon as he shot Slocum. But which direction? Which way would Slocum ride, when he could ride again? How many days would Cash have on him? He'd already had plenty of time to get well away. But he might not go too far. He likely thought that he had killed Slocum. Even if he knew that he had not, he would know that Slocum had been hit hard enough to put him out of commission for a spell. He could be anywhere.

As the days passed by, one by one, Slocum grew steadily stronger. He sat up by himself. He began walking around. He was eating beefsteak and potatoes and biscuits. Doc even brought him a glass of whiskey now and then. He asked for a cigar finally, and Doc told Peggy Sue to give him one. It won't be much longer, Slocum thought, and I'll be out of here.

More and more, he thought about Cash. He tried to use logic to figure out where Cash had gone, but that did not work. Still, he tried. He recalled the things that Cash had done to make him feel the way he was feeling. He considered the way the son of a bitch had drygulched him in the saloon. Some would think that was reason enough to kill the man, but Slocum had already wanted to kill him. He didn't hold the drygulching against Cash. That was a mere impulse of self-preservation. He knew that Slocum was after him.

Sooner or later, one place or another, Slocum told himself, he would find Cash. After that, it was simple. He would kill him. In the future, though, he would be more careful. But who would have thought Cash fool enough to try to kill him in cold blood in front of witnesses like that? Well, now Slocum knew. Cash was running scared, and a frightened man will do most anything. From here on, he told himself, he would have to act as if he were trailing a crazy man, a man that might throw dynamite at him or shoot a cannon. Anything.

The day came at last when Slocum was up and fully dressed. He walked downtown to a store, where he bought himself some cigars and four boxes of .45 shells. He stopped in the saloon for a drink. He was walking back toward Doc Spencer's when he saw Sheriff Vance coming toward him. He stopped to wait. He was getting a little tired anyway.

"I see you're up and around, Slocum," said Vance as he approached.

"First time," said Slocum.

"You going to be ready to ride out of town real soon?"

"Well, it can't be any too soon, Sheriff. It ain't exactly a friendly town, outside of Doc's office."

"Now just what the hell do you mean by that?"

"Think about it, Vance. I ride into town and walk into a saloon and get shot. When I come to, the sheriff's telling me to get out of town. That sound friendly to you?"

He walked around Vance and headed back toward Doc's place. Vance turned and watched him go for a while. Then he went on about his business. Back at Doc's place, Slocum approached Spencer.

"Doc," he said, "how much do I owe you?"

"The bill's not totaled up yet," Doc said. "Why not wait till we're all through here? Then we'll see—"

"I'm moving on now, Doc," said Slocum.

"Now?"

"That's what I said."

"You're not ready for riding, Slocum. And those bandages still need to be changed regular. Hang around a few more days at least."

"Sorry, Doc. I think it's time for me to ride on."

He questioned a few people in town before he left, but all he could find out was that Cash had ridden west. With no more than that to go on, Slocum did the same. He rode out of town going west. He knew that Cash had plenty of time to be far away. Even so, he rode slowly. Doc had been right. He wasn't really ready. But he had been wasting time, and he wanted to be out on the trail again. Occasionally, he passed a traveler, and when he did, he stopped to make small talk and ask about Cash. He had no luck.

For three nights, he slept on the ground and ate beans out of cans, or hardtack, or jerky. Early in the morning of the fourth day, he realized that he was traveling a little faster than before. He was feeling stronger again. Noticeably stronger. That night, he stopped to camp a little early to take advantage of the daylight. After he had taken care of his horse and prepared his camp, he set up some rocks and sticks, and he shot at them with his Colt. He practiced drawing and firing. He was a little slow. He needed the practice.

It was a couple of nights later when he rode into the small town of Broken Leg. There was only one combination saloon, eatery, and store. A penciled sign on the wall advertised rooms out back. There was a small stable next to the place. Slocum wasn't sure if he wanted to stay there for the night or not, but he tied his horse in front of the place, which was called Gorky's, and went inside. There were half a dozen people in there, some eating, some drinking, and others just sitting and visiting. It seemed that Gorky's was the place to be in Broken Leg. Slocum stood looking around, and a short, round-faced man with a mustache and no hair on top of his head came almost rushing at him with a big smile across his face.

"Come in," he said. "Come in. Welcome to Gorky's. There's a nice clean table just over here. You want to sit down?"

Slocum moved toward the table the man had indicated. "Yeah," he said. "I'll sit a spell and have a glass of good bourbon."

"Coming right up," said the little man, and he ran behind a counter to pour the drink. When he brought it back, Slocum noted with pleasure that the squat fellow was generous with his whiskey.

"You serving meals?" he asked.

"I got good beef, pork, even got some quail today. Sometimes, I got fish from the river nearby, but today I got no fish. I have Mexican dishes too: tamales, enchiladas, chiles rellenos. What would you like?"

"How about a good steak?"

"I got it coming right up. You want some potatoes with it? Gravy?"

"Yeah. That'd be good."

Slcoum sipped his whiskey while the little man ran back to get the meal. Casually, he glanced around the room. There was an aging saloon girl, still trying to look young. There were two cowboys. One man had the look of an old gambler. And there was a Mexican vaquero. The vaquero had his own bottle on his table. As Slocum was glancing around the room, the vaquero caught his eye and nodded. Slocum touched the brim of his hat. The vaquero stood up and, bringing his bottle with him, walked over to the table where Slocum sat.

"Pardon me, Señor," he said. "May I sit down?"

Slocum looked at the man a moment. "I guess so," he said. "You just looking for conversation?"

"You are new in this town," the man said.

"I won't be here long enough to need any new friends."

The Mexican laughed. "My name is Gregorio Valenzuela," he said. He extended his hand. Slocum eyed him suspiciously, but shook anyway.

"Slocum," he said.

"Just Slocum?"

"That ought to be enough."

The short man came back with Slocum's meal and put it on the table in front of him. The vaquero looked at the food, then looked up at the short man. "Gorky," he said, "bring me the same thing, will you?"

"Of course, Señor Valenzuela." He rushed off again. Slocum cut into his steak.

"Broken Leg does not get many visitors, Señor Slocum," said Valenzuela.

"I can imagine," said Slocum.

Valenzuela laughed. "Ah, yes. You mean there's not much here to visit. Right?" Slocum did not bother answering that question. He just kept eating. "Well," continued Valenzuela, "it's a nice little town. If little towns are to your taste."

"It don't matter to me one way or the other," said Slocum. "The man's got good food and good whiskey. Does he sell cigars?"

"Yes, he does."

"Then it's all right with me."

Gorky came back with the second meal and put it on the table, and Valenzuela busied himself eating. Slocum was wondering about the Mexican's uninvited visit. Valenzuela could just be gregarious, but he doubted it. He couldn't help but think that the man had some purpose in mind, some reason for imposing his presence. Slocum was the first to finish his meal. He leaned back and sipped his whiskey and studied Valenzuela.

"What's your game, Señor?"

Valenzuela looked up. "I beg your pardon."

"Why did you come over here to meet me?"

"Just being friendly, Señor. That's all."

Maybe I'm getting too suspicious, Slocum thought. After all, the last time I walked into a saloon, I got shot. Well, nearly the last time. Maybe this guy is just tired of the local company.

"You live here?" Slocum asked.

"I live not far," Valenzuela said. "I hang out here a lot."

"Yeah? Well, I'm just drifting through. I might stay the night, though. How are those rooms out back?"

"They're nothing special, but they're decent. You can even lock the door from the inside."

"I guess I couldn't ask for more. You reckon he's got one to spare?"

16

The room was nothing special, just a room with a cot in it and not much else, but Slocum slept well there. In the morning, he was up and back inside Gorky's place. Gorky was already at work preparing breakfasts for a few customers. One of them was the old vaquero, Valenzuela. Slocum headed for an unoccupied table, but Valenzuela interrupted him.

"Señor Slocum, please," he said, "there is room here at my table."

Slocum fought back an impulse to either ignore the man or to refuse his invitation. Never one to gladly rub elbows with a stranger, he was especially in no mood to socialize. For some reason, though, perhaps because he was still weak from his recent ordeal, he walked over to Valenzuela's table and sat down.

"I trust you slept well, Señor," said Valenzuela.

"Well enough," said Slocum.

"Señor Gorky is a Russian," said Valenzuela, "but his best meals are Mexican. I recommend his tamales and beans for breakfast. They are very good."

When Gorky came over to the table, Slocum ordered the tamales and beans but with three eggs fried. Valenzuela ordered tamales and beans. Both men ordered coffee, and Gorky soon brought that. Slocum took a sip right away, almost burning his lips and tongue. He poured some out into the saucer and slurped it. Valenzuela did the same.

"Will you be riding on this morning, Señor?" Valenzuela asked.

"That's my plan," said Slocum.

"I figured as much. There's not much here at Broken Leg to keep a man. Not much besides Gorky's good Mexican food."

"And good whiskey," said Slocum.

"Yes. His good whiskey."

Both men were silent for a while sipping their coffee, and Gorky brought out their breakfasts. After that, they busied themselves with eating. When they were done, Gorky brought out more coffee and refilled their cups. Slocum took a cigar out of his pocket and lit it.

"Señor," Valenzuela said cautiously, "generally it's not polite to ask a man his business. I know that. And generally I am a polite man. But I sense something about you. May I ask where you are riding?"

Slocum looked at Valenzuela through a cloud of blue smoke. He thought for a moment. Hell, it couldn't hurt. He hadn't yet asked any questions about his prey passing through. Why not ask this Mexican?

"I'm looking for someone," he said.

"Ah, I thought as much. May one be so bold as to inquire—"

"He calls himself Cash. Joe Cash. As far as I know, he's well ahead of me. I was laid up for a spell. I'm not even sure that I'm on the right trail now."

"This Cash, he is a friend of yours?"

"He was. Once."

"I might know something about Cash," said Valenzuela. "But I would like to know your intentions regarding him."

"They're simple," said Slocum. "I mean to kill the son of a bitch."

"I too would like to kill the son of a bitch," Valenzuela said.

"Then he's been through here?"

"*Sí*. Not too long ago."

"What did he do?" Slocum asked.

"I had a son, Señor: a very healthy, handsome, promising young man—before Cash came through here."

"How come you let him get away?"

"I was not in Broken Leg when it happened. The word was brought to me just recently, and I am here, ready to go after this man."

"I see," said Slocum.

"And you, Señor? May I ask why you want to kill this man?"

"He shot me," said Slocum. "Without warning. But that's not the main reason. He made me kill a young man, just a kid really."

"Your reasons are strong like mine. Shall we join forces? Shall we see who gets to kill this son of a bitch?"

"Partnering up always seems to end in disaster for me," Slocum said. "I think I'll just go my way."

"If you are on the right trail, Señor, and I think you are, you'll find that almost everyone you meet along the way from here on will be Mexican. You might be able to get some information from them. I know that I can. I also know this country."

"But we don't know that I'm on the right trail."

"Give me just one day, Señor," Valenzuela said, "and I can find out." Slocum looked at Valenzuela again for a long moment. "Waiting one day here to find out for sure will save you time in the long run. Besides, you said that Cash shot you. I can tell that was recently. Another day of rest won't hurt you at all."

"If I wait here a day for you, then you'll want to ride along with me. Is that right?"

"That would be my deal with you, Señor Slocum."

"And when we find Cash?"

"We'll see who can shoot him the quickest."

"All right," said Slocum. "It's a deal. I'll wait here for you till this time tomorrow morning. If you're not back by then, I'm moving on alone."

"That is fair enough, Señor. I'll be on my way."

Valenzuela got up and left Gorky's without any more formalities, and Slocum sat alone wondering if he had made the right decision. In another minute, Gorky came back with the coffeepot.

"You recall a man named Cash?" Slocum asked.

"Oh, yes," said Gorky. "A killer, that one. He killed young Valenzuela. The son of the man you've been talking with. That Cash, he provoked it too."

"Thanks," Slocum said. Gorky had just confirmed everything Valenzuela had told him. Maybe he had made the right choice after all. He wanted his revenge on Cash as bad as ever, but then, so did Valenzuela, and Valenzuela's reason was just as good as Slocum's, maybe better. And two against one was better odds.

Slocum drank some more coffee, then went outside to practice shooting. He was almost back to normal: still a little slow, but not much. He went back inside and had a Mexican lunch. Valenzuela was right about one thing. The Russian's Mexican cooking was his best. For the rest of the day, Slocum hung around the place smoking and drinking coffee. When things got slow, Gorky came around to talk to him. Slocum had supper and decided to switch to whiskey.

He was on his third glass when Valenzuela came back in. He went straight to Slocum's table and sat down. "You're back early," Slocum said. "Have a drink?"

"Sí."

Slocum called for another glass and poured Valenzuela

a drink. The vaquero drank it down and had a second poured.

"You're on the right trail," he said.

"How far?" asked Slocum.

"He's maybe four days ahead of us. But he's not going anywhere just now."

"How could you take a half a day's ride and come back with that information?" Slocum asked.

"I told you, didn't I, that Mexicans live all along the way on this trail? The word passes from one household to the next. I did not have to travel far to find out what we need to know. Cash is staying at a place called Portales. It's a small town, but not so small as Broken Leg. The population is almost all Mexican. Cash has a room in one of the two hotels. He's been seen in the company of Viviano Garcia, a notorious *bandido*. My friends are afraid that he might be joining up with this man."

"He hasn't yet?"

"It seems not."

"Then the faster we can get to him the better," said Slocum. "We don't need to try to tangle with a whole gang of *bandidos*. Not if we can help it."

"I agree. Are you ready to ride?"

"Now? It'll be dark soon."

"I know the trail well. We can ride it safely in the night."

Slocum turned down his whiskey. He dug in his pocket for some change as he stood up.

"All right," he said. "Let's ride."

The two men did not talk as they rode. Now and then, Valenzuela said something about the trail up ahead of them, but that was about all. They passed several small homes along the trail and rode through one small settlement, but by the time they did, it was all rolled up tight for the night. They kept riding. Finally, Valenzuela turned off the trail and pulled up at a small stream.

"We should rest and water the horses," he said. "This is a good place for it."

Slocum dismounted and let the Appaloosa drink. Valenzuela did the same for his mount. Slocum took a cigar out of his pocket and held it out toward Valenzuela, who took it.

"Thank you, Señor," he said.

Slocum took out another for himself, struck a match, and held it out for Valenzuela. Then he used the same match to light his own. He sat down beneath a large tree and leaned back on the trunk. Valenzuela squatted on his haunches.

"Señor Slocum," he said, "you told me that Cash had once been your friend. Will you tell me how that came about?"

"I made a big mistake," Slocum said. "I saved him from a bunch of cowboys who were fixing to hang him for rustling."

"I bet he was guilty."

"Well, right now, I wouldn't bet against it. At the time, I didn't know him from the president of Mexico. I just don't like lynching is all. Well, we rode together for a spell, came to a town, and got jobs at the same ranch. He seemed to be all right."

"I see."

"Then this kid got to following him around, acted like he thought Cash couldn't do anything wrong. Cash took him under his wing. Taught him about roping and shooting. The shooting was what the kid really took to. Well, a range war started up between our boss and a neighbor rancher. Cash and the kid killed some of the neighbor cowhands. The kid seemed to enjoy it. Then he got off with me, just the two of us, and he called me. I wouldn't draw on him. I tried to talk him out of it, but he went for his gun. I had no choice. I had to kill him. I blame Cash for that."

"But why would the young man try to shoot you? You were on the same side, weren't you?"

"I thought so, but later it became clear that Cash had switched sides. I figured maybe he and the kid switched earlier and just never let us know about it. It's the only reason I can think of, other than him just wanting to add to his reputation."

"And then Cash did shoot you?"

"Not right away. We won the war, but Cash ran off. I went after him, on account of the kid. At a town back down the trail, I stepped into a saloon, and there he was, six-gun out and cocked and pointed. He pulled the trigger almost before I had time to recognize him."

"Ah, *caramba.*"

"Say," said Slocum, "why don't we stay here for a little while? Catch a few winks. Any objections?"

"No objections. It's a pretty good idea. A good place for the horses. We don't have to sleep the night away."

They bedded down and slept, but it did not seem long before Valenzuela was poking Slocum awake. They saddled up and hit the trail again. Slocum was wondering about this night travel, but when the sun began to peek over the far western horizon, and Valenzuela suggested they stop at the next house for breakfast, he decided that the vaquero was right. They had a good start, and they had a good place to stop and eat.

The Mexican family knew Valenzuela and welcomed the travelers into their home. They took care of the horses, and they fed Slocum and Valenzuela a good, big breakfast and lots of hot coffee. Valenzuela questioned them a little about Cash in Spanish, and then he told Slocum in English that as far as they knew, Cash was still in Portales, and he had not yet managed to join up with Garcia. Then, he turned back to the family and thanked them in Spanish, and to Slocum he said, "Shall we go?"

In the middle of the day, they came across two riders, dressed like vaqueros but heavily armed. The two were riding toward them, but they stopped as if they were waiting for Slocum and Valenzuela to do the same, to palaver. It would have been difficult to force their way on down the trail past the two, so Slocum and Valenzuela did stop.

"Howdy," said Slocum.

Valenzuela greeted them in Spanish, and the conversation continued in that language. Now and then, Valenzuela told Slocum something in English about what was being said. "They asked where we are going," he said, and then a little later, "They said they like our horses." Slocum did not like the looks of the two. He didn't like the way they grinned and laughed. Then Valenzuela said, "I think we are going to have to kill them. I think they belong to that gang I was telling you about."

Then the Mexican who was directly in front of Slocum said, "Are you talking about Garcia's gang? That was a pretty good guess. We are Garcia's men all right. So you mean to kill us, do you?"

"Why didn't you talk English to begin with?" asked Slocum.

"Why should I? I wasn't talking to you nohow."

Then the two Garcia men went for their guns at almost the same time. Slocum and Valenzuela did the same. A bullet tore through the sombrero on Valenzuela's head, but his own bullet smashed the shoulder of the *bandido* that had fired it. The man screamed in pain, dropping his gun. Valenzuela fired again, knocking him from the saddle and killing him. The other man's bullet missed Slocum completely, and Slocum's return shot hit him in the face. He jerked and twitched in the saddle, and then he relaxed and slipped off to one side.

"And I didn't want to get involved with a gang of *bandidos*," said Slocum.

"Maybe we can still avoid it," said Valenzuela.

He dismounted, and Slocum followed suit. They dragged the two bodies off the trail and into the woods. Then they unsaddled the horses, tossed the saddles into the woods on top of the bodies that were already there, and slapped the horses on their rumps to run them off. They stood in the road, watching the two horses run north.

"Maybe they'll turn around and find their way home," Valenzuela said.

"Maybe," said Slocum.

"If not, no one will ever know what happened to their riders."

"Well, let's just hope that no one knows till we've found Cash and done what we have to do."

"Yes, Señor," said Valenzuela. "We'll be hoping that very much."

17

It was early afternoon when they rode into Portales. They saw no sign of Cash, so they went into the nearest saloon for a drink. Standing at the bar, they were drinking their whiskey when Valenzuela said to Slocum, "Don't look now, but Garcia and some of his pistoleros are at the far corner table."

Slocum raised his eyes and looked in the mirror behind the bar. He saw a table with six tough-looking hombres sitting at it. There were a few others scattered here and there around the saloon. "Okay," he said. "Ask the barkeep if he's seen Cash."

The bartender walked back by, and Valenzuela stopped him. "Pardon me, Señor," he said. "My friend and I are looking for a man."

"Just any man, Señor?"

"A gringo. He dresses in black and calls himself Cash. We heard he was here."

"There has been such a man here."

"Is he still around?"

"I don't know," the bartender said with a shrug. "I haven't seen him today."

"You saw him yesterday?"

"*Sí*. Last night."

"*Gracias*."

The bartender went on his way, and Valenzuela translated the gist of the conversation for Slocum. "That means if he ain't here," Slocum said, "he can't be far ahead."

"That's right. But how do we find out if he has left without hanging around and waiting and wasting our time?"

"Let's find us a place to have some dinner," said Slocum, "and think on that for a while."

He finished off his whiskey, and Valenzuela did the same. Then they turned and walked out of the saloon. Behind them, Garcia and his pistoleros watched them go and whispered to one another.

Slocum and Valenzuela found a place just down the street, and they went inside and had a good, big Mexican dinner. They washed it down with several cups of coffee.

"So are you still thinking on it?" asked Valenzuela.

"Let's check out the stable," said Slocum.

They paid for their meals and left, then walked down the street till they found the stable. The man inside spoke no English, so Valenzuela did the questioning. When he was through talking with the man, he turned away and walked a few steps. Slocum followed him.

"He has Cash's horse," Valenzuela said. "He's somewhere in town." Both men looked warily around the street. They saw no sign of Cash. "But where?"

"Where indeed," said Slocum.

"What do you think we should do?"

"Let's get us a room and then put our horses in the stable here," said Slocum. "But keep your eyes open all the time. If he sees us first, he'll shoot us in the back. Remember that."

"I know, Señor."

They checked into the cheapest hotel in town, took their gear up to the room, and then went back for the horses. Mounting up, they rode them to the stable, where Valenzuela dickered with the man. The deal made, they walked back down the street. They checked each eating place, each saloon, to no avail.

"Where could he be?" Valenzuela asked.

"With a whore," said Slocum. "Hell. He could be anywhere." They walked along a little farther, not saying anything, but watching all around. "Let's go back in that place where Garcia was at," Slocum said.

They made their way back to the place where they had started and went inside again. This time, Slocum bought a bottle, and they took it, with two glasses, to a table and sat down. Slocum could see that Garcia and his henchmen were whispering to one another. He poured two glasses of whiskey and raised one to his own lips.

One of the men at the Garcia table stood up and walked across the room. When he reached Slocum's table, he walked around it. That put him on one side of Slocum, and the other five men at Slocum's back. Valenzuela, however, was facing the five men. It looked like trouble. The man shifted his weight a time or two and hooked his thumbs in his gun belt.

"Good day, gentlemen," he said in careful English. "My name is Viviano Garcia. You are strangers here in Portales."

"*Sí,*" said Valenzuela.

"Oh, mister," said Garcia. "Talk English for the sake of your gringo friend. I am talking English. It's only polite. May I ask what is your business in Portales?"

Slocum had a smart-ass remark in his head, but he decided to hold it back. He recalled his own earlier statement about not wanting to get involved with a gang of *bandidos*. He had one purpose, and one purpose only. That was to get Cash. He did not want to allow anything to get in the way of that purpose.

"My name's Slocum," he said. "My friend here is Gregorio Valenzuela. We came here on the trail of a man."

"Are you bounty hunters then?" Garcia interrupted.

"Maybe you know about the price on my head. Are you thinking about trying to collect it?"

"No," said Slocum. "We don't know anything about that, and we're not interested in you or in bounty."

"In who then, and for why?"

"The man's name is Cash," Slocum said. "We believe he's somewhere in Portales."

"Cash. Cash. Hey, compadres," Garcia said, raising his voice, "do we know someone named Cash?"

The other five *bandidos* all talked at once, saying non-committal things and repeating the name Cash. Finally, they quieted down again.

"Is there a price on the head of this Cash?"

"Not that we know of," said Valenzuela.

"No? Then why are you looking for him? Perhaps he's a friend of yours? Perhaps you're thinking of putting together a gang of pistoleros to compete with Garcia. I don't care for anyone else operating in my territory. You want to settle it now?"

"There's nothing to settle," said Slocum. "We don't mean to put anything together. We're just after Cash. That's all."

"For what?"

"He killed my son," said Valenzuela.

The look on Garcia's face became serious. "Oh," he said. "I see. You mean to kill him for that. I don't blame you. But why is this gringo riding along with you?"

"I want Cash for my own reasons," said Slocum.

"We are both on the same trail," said Valenzuela. "We decided to ride along together."

"I see. Well, perhaps I will find out something for you. Perhaps I will let you know. Are you staying here in Portales?"

"For now," said Slocum.

"You'll be hearing from me," said Garcia, and he walked

back toward the table where his compadres were still seated. His voice very low, Valenzuela said, "He knows where Cash is. There is no doubt about it."

"I figured that," said Slocum.

Back at the corner table, Garcia leaned over toward one of the other five men. "Pedro," he said, "go find Señor Cash. Come back and let me know where he is."

"*Sí*, Viviano."

The man called Pedro got up and walked out of the saloon. Slocum took note of that, but made no move. He and Valenzuela had one more glass of whiskey each. Soon after that, Pedro returned and went back to the Garcia table. He whispered to Garcia, "Cash is with fat Rosita. He has been there for a while. He should be coming out soon."

The other men at the table laughed. When the laughter died down, Pedro said, "There's more, Viviano."

"More?"

"*Sí*. The horses of Pablo and Chico have just come into town. They have no riders and no saddles."

"You're sure they are the horses that Pablo and Chico were riding?"

"*Sí*. I'm sure."

"Then someone has killed them. Go to the stable and check on Señor Cash's horse. Hurry."

Pedro left the saloon again.

"I wonder what's going on with them," Slocum said.

When Pedro returned again, he was puffing for breath. "Cash's horse has not moved for two days," he said.

"Then it was someone else," said Garcia. "Did you see the *caballos* come into town?"

"*Sí*."

"Which direction did they come in from?"

"They came in from the north."

Garcia got up and walked back over to the table where Valenzuela and Slocum were sitting.

"Will you buy me a drink?" he asked.

The bartender put a glass on the bar, and Garcia reached over to pick it up.

"Sit down," said Slocum.

Garcia sat, and Slocum poured his glass full of whiskey.

"Where did you ride in from?" Garcia said.

"From Gorky's at Broken Leg," said Valenzuela.

"Ah, from up north."

"That's right," said Slocum. "What difference does it make?"

"Two of my compadres were riding up north," Garcia said. "Just now, it seems, their horses have come home alone. These two were very good horsemen. I think someone has killed them along the trail—to the north."

"That's too bad," Slocum said. "Do you think we did it?"

"I was thinking maybe you killed them. I don't know why, but there is really no one else. None of the people who live around here would dare to kill any of my pistoleros. It had to be strangers. I thought about your compadre. Cash. But I checked on him. He hasn't been out of town."

"Maybe there's someone else out on that trail that hasn't come into town yet," said Slocum.

"Perhaps," said Garcia. He drank down his whiskey and stood up. "Perhaps."

"Anything could have happened out on that trail," Valenzuela said. "You haven't even seen any bodies."

"You are right about that, amigo," Garcia said. "Maybe they found some whores and were careless and let their horses get away. Maybe their cinch straps broke, both of them at the same time, and they fell off their horses with their saddles. I doubt those things, but maybe it could have been like that. I'll send some men out to look for the bodies, but before I do that, Señor Slocum, I think I will kill you."

Slocum glanced over his shoulder.

"Oh, don't worry about them, Mr. Slocum," said Garcia.

"They know I need no help. They won't move a muscle to help me. Of course, if you should be so lucky as to kill me, then I won't be able to stop them. I think they would kill you then, because they love me so."

"I got no reason to kill you," said Slocum. "Cash's the man I want."

"I don't think you'll live to see him."

Slocum shoved back his chair. Slowly, he stood up and moved away from the table. He managed to move just enough that he could see the other *bandidos* out of the corner of his eye. If he should have to kill Garcia, he knew that he would also have to start shooting at once at the others. He meant to be ready, and he hoped that Valenzuela was as well.

"Well?" said Garcia. "Go for your gun."

"I told you," said Slocum, "I got no reason to kill you."

"Then I will give you one."

Garcia's hand went for his gun, but Slocum was in good form. His own hand flashed, and his Colt was out and cocked and leveled at Garcia's chest by the time Garcia cleared leather. The *bandido* chief stopped short. He stood in a crouch, his revolver out of the holster but pointed at the floor in front of his feet. He smiled. Then he laughed.

"You have beat me, Mr. Slocum," he said. "No one else has ever beat me."

He lowered his gun hand, and then he raised it carefully to drop the gun back into the holster. Slocum, cautious, still held his ready. Garcia raised his hands and walked to the table. He pulled out a chair.

"May I?"

Slocum holstered his Colt. "Go ahead," he said. He waited until Garcia was seated, and then he sat down again.

"May I have another drink?" Garcia asked.

"Help yourself," Slocum said, and Garcia reached for the bottle and poured himself a drink. He took a long swig.

"You know," he said, "I no longer believe that you killed

my two pistoleros. Or if you did, they must have provoked you. You made me look death in the eyes just now, but I'm still alive. Tell me, Slocum, am I alive because you knew that if you killed me, my pistoleros over there would have killed you?"

"Maybe," Slocum said, "but I could have gotten at least two of them before you hit the floor."

"I would have killed the rest," said Valenzuela.

Garcia looked from Slocum to Valenzuela with disbelief in his eyes. Then he started to laugh again. When he stopped laughing, he said, "You know, if you instead of that Cash had come to me, and if you had done me the way you did just now, you would already be my *segundo*."

"Cash came to you?" asked Slocum.

"Oh, yes," said Garcia. "I neglected to tell you. He came to me, wanting to join up with me, but I am cautious with gringos." He looked at Slocum. "Pardon me, Señor," he said. "No offense intended."

"None taken," said Slocum.

"I told him I would think about it. He's been hanging around town ever since, I suppose, waiting for me to make up my mind."

"Where is he?" asked Valenzuela.

"Be patient," said Garcia. "I will see that you get together with him. But will he face both of you?"

"Only one at a time," said Valenzuela. "If he survives the first one."

"And who will be first?"

"I will," Slocum said.

"No," said Valenzuela. "I will try him first."

Slocum started to protest, but Garcia interrupted, putting an end to the argument. "I think, Mr. Slocum," he said, "that you are much too fast for Cash. I think if you face him first, Mr. Valenzuela will never have a chance at his revenge for his poor son. I think I will send for him to meet you, but only if Valenzuela goes first."

18

Slocum and Valenzuela checked their weapons in anticipation of the meeting with Cash, as Pedro once again was launched on an errand. In a short while, Pedro returned. Garcia stopped him beside the table where he sat with Slocum and Valenzuela. "Did you find Cash?" he asked.

"*Sí.*"

"And did you give him the message?"

"*Sí.*"

"What did he say?"

"He say that he will be in the street in front of this saloon at four o'clock. He say that he is not afraid to meet anyone."

"He will only have to meet me," said Valenzuela. "After that, he will meet the devil."

In his room at the hotel, Cash dressed. He slicked his hair and put on his hat. He took up his gun belt and strapped it around his waist. Then he took out the revolver and checked it over carefully. It was fully loaded, and it was working perfectly. He took the watch out of his pocket and checked the time. It was 2:30. At last, he rolled up his belongings in a blanket, picked up the blanket and his saddlebags, and went out of the room. He did not go to the stairs that would lead him down to the lobby of the hotel. Instead, he walked to the far end of the hall, where he opened a door that led out to a small landing and a set of outdoor stairs. These took him down to the alley behind the building. He walked through the alley to the stable and went in through the back door.

He stepped up behind the unsuspecting stableman and, taking out his revolver, banged him over the head, knocking him silly. Moving quickly but cautiously, he located his horse and got him saddled and ready to ride. Then he threw a loop over the neck of Slocum's big Appaloosa. The horse protested, but there wasn't much he could do. Cash did not know the horse of the other man, that Valenzuela. In fact, he did not know the man. All he knew was that Pedro had told him that Slocum and a man named Valenzuela were waiting for him. That was all.

Cash looked over all the stalls very quickly and discovered that there were only four more horses in there. He put ropes on them all. Mounted up, he rode past each stall, opening the gate and holding the lead rope, then rode out through the back door while leading all the horses with him. This would slow his pursuers considerably. After he had gone a few miles away from Portales, he would turn the animals loose. They would slow him down and get in his way. But at first, he needed them, or actually, he needed to be sure that Slocum and Valenzuela did not have them.

Cash rode out of Portales through the alley, and he rode in a direction that would not take him past the saloon where the two men waited along with the Garcia gang. He rode slowly, making as little noise and calling as little attention to himself as possible. Once out of town, he rode hard for a few miles. Then he slowed again and went on for a few more miles. At last, he turned loose all the horses except the Appaloosa. That one he tied to a tree beside the road. Then he rode on his way.

Four o'clock came and went, and although Valenzuela waited patiently and alone in the street, there was no sign of Cash. Slocum was inside, looking out the window. At 4:15, he looked back at Garcia.

"The son of a bitch ain't coming," he said.

"He told my man that he would be here," Garcia said.

"It's not the first time he's lied," said Slocum.

He walked to the front door and on out onto the sidewalk. Valenzuela looked over his shoulder to see him. "He's not coming, Valenzuela," said Slocum. He kept walking. Garcia and all his men came out of the saloon and followed Slocum. Valenzuela fell in step. Slocum went straight to the stable and inside. There, he found the man that Cash had clobbered on the head. The poor wretch was still out cold. He also saw at once that all the stalls were empty.

"Damn it," he shouted.

"Our horses are gone," said Valenzuela.

Garcia turned on Pedro. "What's the meaning of this?" he said.

Pedro backed off a couple of steps, shrugging as he backed. "I don't know," he said. "The man told me he would be in the street."

Slocum stood up from where he had knelt beside the stable man. "Someone had better get a doctor for this man," he said, but he did not stop to see if anyone had paid any attention to what he had said. He walked to the back door of the stable, which was still standing wide open, and checked the tracks. They had all gone out that way, and then they'd continued out of town. His Appaloosa was among them.

"All bets are off," he said. "I'll kill that son of a bitch the next time I see him."

"You still have to beat me to him," said Valenzuela.

"And now you have to beat me as well," said Garcia. "Let's get going."

"On what?" asked Valenzuela.

"Pedro and Pancho will stay behind," Garcia said. "You and Slocum can take their horses. They are all tied back at the saloon. Come on."

Soon Slocum, Valenzuela, Garcia, and three of Garcia's pistoleros were riding the trail after Cash. For a few miles out of Portales, the road was tree-lined. Then the trees grew more scarce, and the terrain began to roll with low gradual hills. The hills then grew steeper, and on the sides of the road, large rocks rose up. They had not gone far into the rocky hills before they spotted the horses that Cash had turned loose. Garcia ordered one of his men to take them back to Portales. That left Slocum, Valenzuela, Garcia, and two men following Cash. In another couple of miles, they found the Appaloosa tied to a tree beside the road. Slocum switched the saddle from the horse he was riding to the Appaloosa's back and climbed aboard.

"It ain't your own saddle, ole pard," he said, "but it'll have to do for now."

Soon it was too dark to continue safely. The road was unfamiliar even to Garcia. They decided to stop for the night. As they sat around a small fire, wishing they had some coffee and beans at least, Garcia said to Slocum, "This Cash is one no-good coward. I am fortunate that I did not accept him into my ranks."

"Don't let him fool you," said Slocum. "I've seen him stand up to a man and gun him. He's not a coward. He's just practical. That's all."

"Practical," said Garcia, musing to himself.

"This time we must not let him slip through our fingers," said Valenzuela. "We made that mistake at Portales. This time we must stop him."

"We'll get the son of a bitch," said Slocum.

They bedded down for the night and slept hungry as best they could. In the morning, they rose and got an early start. In a couple of hours, they came to a small wayside inn, and they stopped and had breakfast and eggs. They learned that Cash had gone through the night before. They did not linger over coffee. They were in a hurry to catch Cash. Somewhat refreshed, they were back on the road in a short time.

As the road narrowed, climbing higher into mountains, one of Garcia's men spoke to him. "I think it's not so safe for you here," the man said. "There's a reward for you, and there are posters out. I myself have seen them. The sheriffs over here are looking for you."

"They won't expect me to come riding through," Garcia said. "Don't worry."

At the top of the next rise, a rifle shot rang out, then two more followed in quick succession. Valenzuela fell out of his saddle. Slocum jumped for cover, and so did Garcia, but Garcia's two pistoleros fell, both hit. Slocum was behind a rock on one side of the road, Garcia on the other. Each man had his six-gun out. The rifles were still in the saddle boots.

"You see anything, Garcia?" Slocum called out.

"Not a thing," Garcia answered. "Damn it to hell. The gringo son of a bitch has killed three good men."

"I'm not killed," said Valenzuela, lying still in the middle of the road. "I'm hurt, but not killed."

Slocum was scouring the mountainside. "Where is that bastard?"

"I still don't see no sign of him," said Garcia.

"Be still out there, Valenzuela," Slocum said. "We can't make a move for you right now, and if he sees you move, he'll likely shoot again."

"Don't worry for me," said Valenzuela. "I won't move."

They stayed there under cover for a long time—it seemed to Slocum at least an hour—with poor Valenzuela lying there in the road bleeding. Slocum had no idea how badly Valenzuela was hurt. No more shots were fired. That could be because Cash had no target. He could be waiting the same as they were. At last, Slocum decided that it was time to do something.

He stood up slowly, watching the rocks above him, waiting for a shot. None came. "Garcia," he said. "I think the son of a bitch is gone."

"Don't be too sure, Señor."

"I'm going to get Valenzuela out of the road."

"I'll watch for you."

Slocum moved on out to where Valenzuela was lying. He holstered his six-gun and took Valenzuela under the arms to drag him over to the side of the road behind a small boulder. Still, no shots were fired. He checked the wound.

"It's not too bad," Valenzuela said, but his voice was weak.

"It's bad enough," said Slocum. He started doing what he could for the wound. Garcia got up and crossed the road to join them there.

"I think you are right," he said. "I think the son of a bitch is gone."

"Well, he slowed us down enough," said Slocum.

"And he narrowed the odds against him."

"Yeah. He'll be satisfied for now. He can get more distance between us."

"Well, I've got the bleeding stopped," Slocum said. "That's about all I can do. We need to get him to a doctor."

"The nearest doctor is back at Portales," Garcia said.

"Go on after Cash," said Valenzuela. "Leave me here. I'll be all right."

"We're not leaving you here like this," said Slocum. "Forget it."

"I'll take him back, Señor," said Garcia. "You can go on after that Cash."

Slocum thought a moment. "All right," he said. "Let's get everything ready."

They caught up all the horses, loaded the two bodies on theirs and Valenzuela on his. Garcia then mounted up. Slocum climbed on his Appaloosa.

"Take good care of him, Garcia," he said.

"I will, Señor."

"Slocum," said Valenzuela. "When you have killed Cash, come back to Portales and let me know, will you?"

"I will, Valenzuela. My saddle's back there in the stable anyhow."

"*Vaya con Dios,*" Valenzuela said.

"The same to you," said Slocum, and he spurred the Appaloosa forward.

Slocum did not look back. Instead, he kept searching the high rocks. He found a place up there that looked like a good spot for an ambush, and he rode slowly, looking for a way up. At last he found a narrow passageway that seemed to wind its way up toward the top of the mountain. He turned into it and started up. About halfway up, he pulled his Winchester out of the boot. He kept going.

At last he came to the end of the passageway, and he stopped to dismount. There was a natural hiding place there. He walked over to check it out, and he found three spent shells lying in the dirt. It was the place of ambush all right. It was where Cash had stopped to wait for them. But where had he gone? Slocum had not heard any sound of hooves coming down the mountain. The passageway was not that far from where they had been hit. He looked around some more. There was a pile of rocks behind him that looked suspicious.

Climbing up over the rocks, he saw that the trail he had come up continued on the other side. He saw the tracks of a horse and footprints made by a man. How could that be? A horse would not be able to climb over that mess. He studied the rocks some more. At last he decided that Cash had discovered the trail, gone to the top and found his hiding place, taken his horse on over the top of the trail, and then pushed the rocks down to block the trail. When he was ready to make his escape, all he had to do was climb over the pile of rocks and mount his horse. In order to follow him, Slocum would have to move the pile of rocks one at a time.

Cash had really slowed him down. Well, hell, he thought, there's nothing else for it. He picked up a rock and tossed it aside. Then another and another. He had to stop and rest and wipe the sweat from his brow a time or two. At last he reached the trail. It was clear enough to ride through. He sat down for a moment to catch his breath. Then he got up and mounted his Appaloosa. He rode on over the crest of the mountain.

Cash's trail was clear from there. Likely, he did not think he would be followed. He thought either that he would have killed them all or that they would not be able to figure out his trick at the top of the mountain. If Slocum was right, then Cash would be relaxed, unsuspicious. He should be able to slip up on him with some ease. He kept riding down the steep mountain trail. At the bottom of the trail at last, he found himself on a road again. He looked back to see the road curve. He looked up at the mountain trail he had just negotiated.

Damn, he thought. It looks to me like I've just come back down to the same damn road I was on in the first place. Cash, Slocum figured, was far sneakier than he had been giving him credit for. Looking down in the road, he checked the tracks once more. They continued in the same direction as they had been going in the first place. He rode on.

In about a mile, he came to a house by the side of the road, and he stopped. The door opened, and a Mexican man stepped out. Slocum touched the brim of his hat. "Do you speak English?" he asked.

The man gave a shrug.

"Oh, boy," said Slocum under his breath. Then out loud, he said, "Uh, *agua. Por* my *caballo*?"

"Oh, *sí*," said the man with a smile. He pointed to a trough nearby, and Slocum rode to it and dismounted, allowing the Appaloosa to drink freely.

"Gracias," he said. "I'm looking for someone. Oh, *un hombre* dressed all in *negro. Hombre. Negro.*"

The man smiled again and nodded his head. Slocum took that to mean that Cash had been by, and the man had seen him. He thought about trying to find out how long ago that had been, but despaired of trying it. He reached into a pocket and pulled out a coin, which he flipped to the man. *"Gracias,"* he said. He mounted up and turned back onto the road. Behind him, he could hear the little man calling after him, *"Gracias, señor. Gracias, señor."*

Over the next hill, he was astonished to see a city laid out before him. That would make it the more difficult to locate Cash, he thought. He cursed and rode on in. As he reached the outskirts, he met a man on horseback.

"Howdy," he said.

"Howdy."

"You see a man in black ride by here?"

"No. Sure ain't."

"Just one more thing, pard," said Slocum. "Can you tell me where the hell I am?"

19

"Why, hell, stranger, you're in Cow Town."

Slocum pointed toward the city ahead. "And that there—"

"That there is El Paso."

Slocum rode on down into the city and found a saloon. At the bar, he bought himself a drink. He had one more, and then he went out to look up a stable for his Appaloosa and a hotel room for himself. No one he spoke to admitted to having seen Cash. In his room, he poured out all his cash, and he discovered that he did not have much left. He could spend another night or two in the room and eat his meals for those few days, have a few drinks. That would just about take care of it. Now he had to think about finding some work, but if he got himself a job, that would allow Cash to put that much more distance between them. Well, he'd sleep on it. Maybe in the morning he would wake up with a nice clear head, and the world would look like a totally different place.

He woke up the next morning with a belly grumbling hunger, and he recalled that he had not had any supper the night before. If his head was any clearer than it had been, it was only because the awful hunger had shoved everything else out. He couldn't think of anything else. He dressed hurriedly and went downstairs. There was a café in the hotel, and rather than waste time looking for a better place, he went in there. He ordered flapjacks, bacon, eggs, potatoes, and coffee. After he had finished it all, he ordered it all over again.

At last, with his belly overfull, he got up to pay his bill. The amount astonished him. It took almost all the money he had left. He could not afford even one more night in the hotel. He should have gone out looking for a cheaper place to eat. He thought that he could kick himself in the ass for what he had done, but it was too late to do any good. He had blown away most of his cash. He tried to console himself by thinking about how good it felt to be full, but when he did that, all he could think of was that in a few hours he would be hungry again.

He went back to his room and packed up what little gear he had in there. Then he checked out of the room and took the gear to the stall housing his horse. He did have enough to pay for the stable. He would have to be careful and hold that much out. He knew that if he stuck around the damn city, he would want another drink or two come evening. Damn it, he thought, he would have to look for work. He had no choice. If Cash was still running, he would just get farther ahead. That's all there was for it.

He decided to stop in the sheriff's office and ask his questions. He had to do something and do it fast. The sheriff was in. He was a tall slender man, dressed in a three-piece suit that looked to Slocum to be much too hot for this south Cow Town country. The man was in his thirties, and he sported a mustache that covered his mouth and chin. He looked up from his paperwork when Slocum walked in.

"I know you," he said.

Slocum was taken aback. He did not recognize the man. As far as he knew, he had never seen him before.

"Well, you got the advantage of me, mister," he said.

"You're Slocum. John Slocum."

"Yeah. I know that."

"I'm Festus Platero. Sheriff here."

They shook hands, and Platero offered Slocum a chair and a cigar. Slocum took them both and lit the cigar, but he was puzzled. "You, uh, you don't have any dodgers on me, do you?" Slocum asked.

Platero laughed. "No. I got none. Why? Should I have?"

"Far as I know, I'm not wanted for anything in Cow Town. Not just now. But how come you know who I am?"

Platero laughed again. "I was in Fort Worth about five, six, year ago when you killed those three worthless cowboys from Kansas. I don't recollect their names. In fact, I probably never heard them in the first place. It was a dazzling display of gunmanship."

"I don't remember you," Slocum said.

"No reason you should. I was standing by watching. That's all. But it made a fine and lasting impression on me. Well, what brings you here?"

"I'm looking for a man," said Slocum. "Thought maybe you could help me."

"Has he got a name?"

"Joe Cash."

"I ran him out of town two days ago," said Platero.

"Which way'd he go?"

"You mean to join up with him or kill him?"

Slocum thought long and hard before answering. "I mean to kill him," he said finally.

"I can tell you where he went, Slocum, but I ain't going to. Not just yet."

"How come?"

"I need a favor. If you'll do a little job for me, I'll tell you what you want to know. I'll even pay you for doing the job." Slocum sat silent, waiting for more. A little cash in his pockets would be all right. "What do you say?" Platero continued.

"What's the chore?" Slocum asked.

"There's a man called Gear that has a place just across the line in Mexico. He's a white man, though. An American. He's got some stolen horses down there, and I can't go after them on account of the jurisdictional thing, you know. I can't go after them, but I want them back in the worst way. They're the property of a real important fellow here in El Paso. It would be worth, say, a hundred dollars to me to get those horses."

"What about Gear?"

"I don't care about him one way or the other. Hell, you could have the job done and the money in your jeans by nightfall if you was to get right after it."

"Give me the details," Slocum said.

Slocum found Gear's place, all right. It was a small adobe not far from the river. A corral behind the house held seven fine-looking horses. Slocum studied the layout for a time. If the seven horses all belonged to the man in El Paso, then Gear wasn't home. Or he was out for a long walk. This promised to be too easy. Something about it bothered Slocum, but he couldn't pin it down. He decided to liberate the stolen horses and drive them home.

The river was behind the adobe, and there was a grove of trees off to the left about a hundred yards. There wasn't much else. He could see for a long ways. He rode down to the house and called out. No one answered. He dismounted and walked in. There was no one home, just as he figured. He went out and got back in the saddle. Riding around to the corral, he opened the gate and started the horses along. Then all hell broke loose.

Where the hell had they come from? It was as if they rose up out of the ground or materialized out of the dry air. There were four of them, but Slocum wasn't counting. They were on all sides of him, and they were shooting. One bullet knocked the hat from his head, and another tore his left side. He flung himself off his horse, drawing his Colt at the same time. His first bullet found its mark, dropping one of the men in his tracks. Slocum rolled under the feet of the upset horses. He looked in another direction and snapped off a shot that broke the back of a second man. Then he was on his feet, looking over the back of one of the stamping, milling horses for another target. Someone grabbed him around the shoulders from behind.

"I got him, Freddie," the assailant screamed. "Come on."

The one called Freddie suddenly materialized in front of Slocum, who was busy trying to shake the other one off his back. When Slocum saw Freddie approaching, he stopped struggling and raised up his Colt. He could only raise it as high as his waist, for the man had his arms pinned to his sides from behind. But it was enough. He fired, and Freddie jerked and twitched and growled and fell forward on his face.

Then Slocum spread his feet apart, pointed the Colt between his legs, and shot the final man in the right foot. The man yowled and turned him loose. He hopped around on his good foot, screaming and howling until he fell over on his ass. He held the wounded appendage in both hands. Somewhere along the way, he had dropped his weapon. Slocum looked at the wretch and thought about killing him, but there was no sense in it. Instead, he found the revolver the man had dropped. He picked it up and tossed it away. He looked around. There were three bodies, and this wounded man. The seven horses had scattered, but he could still see them all. It would just take some time to round them up again.

Then, for the first time, Slocum saw some holes that had been dug in the ground around the corral. So that was the secret of the sudden appearance of these men. They had been hiding in holes in the ground. So once again, if the seven horses indeed belonged to the man in El Paso, then where were the four horses these men had ridden? He looked at the man sitting and sobbing in the dirt in front of him.

"You blowed my foot off," the man accused. "You might as well go on ahead and shoot me dead."

"I don't think so," said Slocum. "Are you Gear?"

"Hell, no. He was the first one you kilt."

Slocum thought for a minute, and then he remembered something he had seen in the adobe. He walked over to it and went inside. Taking a bottle of tequila off a shelf, he walked back out to the corral. He uncorked the bottle, took a swig, corked it again, and tossed it to the man. "Here," he said. "Pour some on your foot and drink the rest."

He reloaded his six-gun, remounted his horse, and set about rounding up the seven animals he had come after. It took a good part of the day, but he got them together again. The man in the yard was still just sitting there, drinking tequila, and now and then shouting obscenities at Slocum. Slocum drove the horses across the river and headed them for the sheriff's office in El Paso. It was late in the day when he got them delivered, but Platero was still there. He came out of the office, smiling and counting out some bills, which he handed to Slocum. Slocum tucked them in his pocket and dismounted.

"I see you got them all," Platero said.

Slocum shot out a right that caught Platero on the jaw and knocked him on his ass right there in the street in front of his office. Platero sat up astonished and rubbed his jaw.

"What the hell was that for?"

"That was for sending me out on a hundred-dollar job to gather a few horses, knowing all along I'd have to kill some men to do it."

"You go to stealing a man's stock," Platero said, standing up slowly, "you got to expect some resistance from him."

"You don't expect men to come crawling out of holes in the ground. It was an ambush. Carefully planned. And it was either for you or for the owner of these horses."

"And you think I knew about it?"

"You had a pretty good idea, you son of a bitch," Slocum said. "And now you still owe me something."

"What's that?"

"Where's Cash?"

"Oh, yeah. I'll tell you over a drink."

"What about these horses?"

Platero waved an arm and called to a man on the sidewalk. "Take care of these horses," he said. "Will you?" The man agreed. Platero looked back at Slocum. He pointed toward the nearest saloon. "Over there," he said. They started to walk toward the saloon together.

"You're buying," said Slocum.

"Fair enough."

Inside the saloon, Platero got a bottle and two glasses and led the way to an empty table. The two men sat down, and Platero poured the glasses full. They drank them down, and he refilled them.

"Well?" said Slocum. "I didn't come in here just to be sociable with you."

"No, you didn't, did you? Although I do admire to be sitting here and having a friendly drink with you. You were truly inspirational to me, Slocum. Now, you've done it again. Killed four men this time."

"Three," Slocum corrected.

"Just three?"

"The fourth one's got a hole in his right foot."

"And you left him alive?"

"Why not?"

Platero shrugged. "Well," he said, "I wish I could tell you that Cash was still here, but he rode out."

"You told me you ran him out of town two days ago," Slocum said. "All I want to know is which way did he go."

"He headed for the Cow Town hill country," said Platero. "That's all I can tell you. Hillsboro maybe. Someplace like that."

"How'd you come by that information?"

"He talked loose in the saloon," Platero said. "To the gals, even to some of the cowhands. They told me."

Slocum downed his drink and started to get up.

"Hey," said the sheriff. "What's your hurry? It's too late to start out on his trail tonight. We've got damn near a whole bottle of whiskey here to finish."

"I've had all I want," said Slocum. He walked out of the saloon and got his Appaloosa. He left the horse in the stable and went back to the hotel. He had money again. He checked himself back in and went up to the room to get some sleep. As he lay in bed, staring at the ceiling, he could not seem to drop off. He considered the way in which he had been used by Platero. The son of a bitch had known there would be an ambush, and he had sent Slocum into it without telling him. Of course, he had paid reasonably well for the job, but Slocum would have liked it better had the bastard been straight with him from the beginning.

Oh, well, what the hell? He had a hundred bucks on him. He was in a nice hotel room. His horse was being looked after, and after they'd both had a good night's rest, they would be on Cash's trail again in the morning. If he could just get to sleep. God damn but it had been a bloody trail. He had met outlaws and lawmen, and damned if some of the outlaws hadn't been the better men. He got to thinking about Garcia, and then he thought about Valenzuela. He hoped that Garcia had gotten the old boy to a doctor in time to do some good.

When this business was all over with, Slocum resolved, he would go back to Portales and find Valenzuela, if he was still alive, and tell him what had happened. Hell, he might even take him Cash's head. Maybe his ears at least. He decided that he was thinking morbid thoughts, and he had better put them out of his mind. He'd try to think about women. That should do the trick. But the first one that came into his mind was Julie Townsend, and that was more distasteful to him than was the thought about Cash's ears. At last, he drifted off to sleep.

In the morning, he dressed and packed quickly. He wanted to be out of El Paso and on the trail again. He wanted to hurry up and bring this thing to a close. He went downstairs and walked up to the counter.

"Yes, sir?" said the clerk.

"I'm checking out," said Slocum, reaching for his money. Then he hesitated. He stopped fishing in his pockets. He looked at the clerk and said, "Send the bill to the sheriff's office."

20

For the next few weeks, Slocum wandered from one small town to another, and it seemed that everywhere he went, Cash had been there, but he had left two or three days before. He was always just ahead. Now and then, Slocum discovered, Cash had killed someone in the town just before leaving. He was not leaving behind any friends. That much was certain. Before too long, Slocum's money was running out again. At last, he found himself at Orvel Patterson's Switchback Ranch, busting broncs to line his pockets again. He would save up a little more money and get back on the trail of Cash.

He had just ridden a real ring-tailed cayuse to a standstill, and he was feeling battered as hell. That tough little son of a bitch had beat him nearly to a pulp. He kicked it in the sides and rode it calmly around the corral a few times. Then he dismounted, unsaddled the creature, and let it go. He hobbled over to the corral fence and tossed the saddle over the top rail. He bent over with a groan and slipped through the top and middle rails to get outside the corral. He was about to head toward the bunkhouse, walking with a list to one side, when a young cowboy called Martin came riding up.

"How you doing, Mr. Slocum?"

"Feeling kind of old," Slocum said.

Martin swung down out of the saddle. "I'd like to talk to you," he said.

Slocum stopped walking. "What is it?" he asked.

"I got to turn this horse loose first. You going to be around?"

"I'll be in the bunkhouse," Slocum said.

"I'll see you there in just a few minutes. Okay?"

"Sure. Come on ahead. I won't be doing anything. Just recovering is all."

As he limped his way on over to the bunkhouse, Slocum wondered what the young fellow wanted to talk to him about. Surely not about bronc riding. He couldn't think what it could be. He went on inside to his bunk, sat down, pulled off his boots, and then stretched himself out with a moan. That damn cayuse had been his fourth that day. He was really worn out. He closed his eyes, and thought that he was about to drift off, when he heard Martin's footsteps coming in, and a moment later, his voice.

"Mr. Slocum?"

Slocum looked up. "Yeah. What's on your mind, young feller?"

Martin sat on the bunk next to Slocum's and twirled his hat in his hands nervously. He did not look directly at Slocum. "Mr. Slocum," he said, "I don't rightly know how to ask this, but I— Well, some of the boys has been saying that you're a gunfighter. Is that true?"

"What kind of a question is that to ask a man?"

"I'm sorry. I know it ain't polite. But I'm needing some advice, and I—"

"Just tell me about it," Slocum said.

"Well, all right. I will. I was in town this morning, and I run into a feller. I hadn't never seen him before. Didn't know him, and he didn't know me. Well, cutting through all the bullshit, he kinda pushed me, and I called him on it.

Now I'm supposed to meet him out by Boot Hill this evening to have it out. You know, a shoot-out. He looked and
talked like a gunfighter. I wasn't wearing no gun. That's
how come we're to meet later. I said I'd get my gun. I know
I shouldn't have let him push me into it, but I— Well, there
was several guys hanging around listening to ever'thing
that was said. Before I knew what I was doing, I'd agreed
to meet him."

"Well, you let yourself get suckered, kid, but I don't
know what I can do for you. What do you want from me?"

"I—I don't know. Hell, I shouldn't even have brought it
up, I guess. I just went and got myself into something I hadn't
oughta. I guess I'll just have to find my own way out of it. Or
get myself killed. I'm sorry I bothered you, Mr. Slocum."

Martin stood up, put his hat on his head, and started to
walk away, but Slocum sat up and stopped him. "Hold on,
boy," he said.

Martin turned back. "Yes, sir?"

"First thing, stop calling me mister."

"Okay."

"Now, you went and got yourself caught up in a gunfight
with a real gunfighter. Right? Now you're scared, but you
can't back out."

"Yeah. I guess that's about the size of it."

"How are you with a gun?"

Martin shrugged. "I guess I can handle one all right. I
mean, I can knock a can off a fence post. But I ain't no fast
draw. Hell, I never pulled a gun on a man. Never."

"Try to keep the sun at your back," Slocum said. "That
way, it will be in his eyes. Whatever you do, don't let him
get you facing the sun. Don't try to beat him to the draw either. Just make sure that you draw your gun and hit what
you aim at. More often than not, the man who gets his gun
out in a real big hurry is so busy being fast, he misses his
first few shots. Has to empty his six-gun to kill a man. The
main thing is to try to stay calm."

"Thank you. I'll remember that."

"I wish I could help you more, kid, but it was kind of short notice. We ain't got time for shooting lessons."

"Yeah. Well, I just met that son of a bitch this morning. Cocky. Just itching to kill someone, I think. All dressed in black too, and—"

"What?" said Slocum. "Hold on. Dressed in black, you say?"

"Yeah. He was. All in black. Everything."

Slocum stood up and walked toward Martin. Suddenly, there was a look in his eyes that froze the blood in the boy's veins. He put his hands on Martin's shoulders and looked him straight in the eyes. "This gunslick," he said, "did he have a name?"

"Called himself Cash."

Slocum's arms dropped to his sides as he heaved a heavy sigh of relief from all the long searching, all those times he rode into town to hear that Cash was two or three days gone. All that long trail he had ridden, and all the bodies that Cash had left along the way. He took a deep breath and tried to remain calm.

"Boy," Slocum said, "when you get ready to ride over to Boot Hill to meet up with Cash, I'm going to ride along with you."

"You mean it?"

"You're damn right."

"Well, I— I appreciate it, Mr., uh, Slocum."

"It's all right."

"Say, do you know this man?"

"I know him," Slocum said. "Just let me know when you're ready to ride."

"I will."

Martin left the bunkhouse, and Slocum started pacing the floor. He was anxious to get on the way to the meeting. At last, he had caught up with Cash. Or Cash had caught up with him without knowing it. In any case, Cash was in town, and apparently had no idea that Slocum was anywhere near. Slocum told himself to calm down. He had been on Cash's trail for so long that a short wait wasn't going to make any difference. But he felt like a man who was near the end of his road and had only two miles left to ride. It was the longest two miles he had ever seen.

He went back to the bunk and stretched out again. He would have to force himself to relax, take it easy, but he was anxious. There was no denying that. He was no longer thinking about his sore muscles and tired bones. There was no room in his mind for anything other than Cash. He did not sleep. He lay there thinking until Martin showed up again. It was early evening.

"It's about time for me to be heading over there," Martin said.

Slocum sprang up from his bunk. "Let's saddle up," he said.

He did not saddle his Appaloosa. He saddled a brown horse from the remuda. He did not want to call attention to himself, did not want Cash spotting him from a distance and running away again. The cemetery was on a flat piece of ground with a grove of trees nearby, and Slocum and Martin were the first ones to arrive. They tied their horses at the grove, and Slocum melted into the trees. They could see the town, but there was no one nearby. On the other hand, Martin stepped out from the trees to make sure that he was seen. He did not want Cash telling it around that he had chickened out.

Soon they could see a rider coming from town. It took a couple of minutes, but then they knew that he was coming their way. In another couple of minutes, they could recognize him. It was Cash, all right. Slocum's heart pounded with anticipation. He did not even pay attention to the kid, who was nervous as hell, contemplating the end of his own young life. Slocum pressed himself against the trunk of a tree, hiding in the shade. Cash rode on up close and dismounted.

"I didn't think you'd show, kid," he said.

"I'm here."

Slocum stepped out in the clear. "So am I," he said.

Cash's jaw dropped. "Slocum," he said. He tried to laugh. "It's been a while, ain't it?"

"It's been a while," Slocum agreed.

"Well, what are you doing here?"

"I came to take this young feller's place, Cash. Step aside, kid."

"Hold on," Cash said. "I ain't going to fight two of you."

"Kid," Slocum said, "take off your gun belt and toss it over yonder."

Martin hesitated, but he did as Slocum told him, tossing the gun belt and gun a good ways away from himself.

"Just me, Cash," said Slocum.

"Hell, Slocum, we're old pards. We don't need to fight it out."

"You switched sides in the war with the White Hat outfit."

"That was just a job."

"You caused me to kill that kid. He forced it, but it was you that put him up to it."

"Now, Slocum, he done that on his own. I swear it."

"You killed young Valenzuela, and you ambushed us on the road. Shot his pa up."

"Was you with that bunch? Hell, I didn't know it. How could I?"

"That's enough talk, Cash. I saved your neck once. It was a big mistake. I mean to make it right today."

"No," said Cash. "No, you don't. You see, I ain't going to draw against you."

"You'll draw. After I shoot off your fucking ears."

"No. No, I won't. And the kid here can forget that we had this meeting. I'm forgetting our differences. I'm fixing to turn my back on you, Slocum, and I'm going to walk back over to my horse and mount up and ride out of here.

I'm going to turn my back, and you won't shoot me in the back. I know you, boy."

He was grinning. He slowly turned around, his back to Slocum. Slocum watched him. Martin was looking from one man to the other, amazed at what he was witnessing. Cash took slow steps toward his horse.

"I'm leaving, Slocum," he said. "Hey, maybe we'll cross paths again somewhere along the way, old pard."

Suddenly, Slocum pulled out his Colt. He pointed it at Cash's back. He pulled back the hammer, and Cash flinched and stopped walking when he heard the ominous *click, click.*

"You won't do it," he said, and he started to walk again.

Slocum waited a few more steps. Cash was about to reach his horse. Slocum squeezed the trigger, and his slug tore into Cash's back between the shoulder blades. Cash jerked with the impact of the bullet. He tried to turn around to face Slocum, but halfway, his knees buckled, and he fell to the ground. He was still alive. He could still try to shoot back. Slocum walked toward him, his Colt held ready. He looked down to see Cash's astonished expression.

"I didn't believe you'd do it," Cash began. "I didn't think you had the—"

"Die, you cold-blooded son of a bitch," Slocum said.

"I—I—"

Cash never finished his last thought. He crumpled up into a wretched-looking black heap on the ground. Slocum said, "It's finished." He knelt down and unbuckled Cash's gun belt. Then he pulled it loose from around the waist of the corpse. He walked back to his horse and hung the two-gun belt on his saddle horn. He turned and looked back in the direction of the body. The astonished kid was staring at him in disbelief.

"Go pick up your gun belt, kid," Slocum said.

The young cowboy ran to get his gun. He strapped it back around his waist. He looked up at Slocum once more.

"Get on out of here," Slocum said.

Martin hurried to his horse, mounted up, and rode away fast, leaving Slocum staring at the body of Joe Cash.

Slocum rode into Broken Leg and, coming close to Gorky's, he could see two horses tied in front. He did not recognize the two horses, but he did recognize the saddle on one of them. It was the saddle he had seen on Viviano Garcia's horse. So the old bandit was in there with some-one else, one of his *bandidos* perhaps. Well, Garcia could tell him about Valenzuela. Slocum dismounted at the rail and tied the Appaloosa. Then he took a burlap bag loose from his saddle, and he walked to the door, opened it, and stepped inside. Gorky saw him at once and smiled.

"You're back," he said. "Welcome back. Come in. Come in."

Slocum's eyes adjusted slowly from the brightness of the sun outside to the darkness inside, and then he saw Garcia seated at a table with a bottle and a glass, and seated there with him was Gregorio Valenzuela. He walked toward them.

"Señor Slocum," said Valenzuela, standing up and smiling.

Garcia did not stand up. He turned and looked over his shoulder, his face wearing a wide grin. "Come and sit down with us and have a drink," he said.

Valenzuela pointed toward the counter, where Slocum's saddle was perched. "We have kept it here for you," he said. "We knew you'd be back."

"I'm glad to see you up and well, Valenzuela," said Slocum. "I've brought something for you."

He took the bag by a corner and turned it upside down, shaking it. Its contents fell out onto the floor and rolled over between Valenzuela's feet. The old vaquero looked down in astonishment at the dull eyes, the drooping mus-tache, and the long now-stringy hair of the head that had once belonged to Joe Cash, the murderer of his son.

Watch for

SLOCUM'S FOUR BRIDES

347th novel in the exciting SLOCUM
series from Jove

Coming in January!